Thank Goodness for Poisonous Snails

Thank Goodness for Poisonous Snails

(A Devilly Peen Murder Mystery)

E.K. Wicher

EKWicherbooks
1400 rue Archambault
Sainte-Adèle
Quebec J8B 2X6
Canada

ISBN 978-1-7774547-4-6 (Paperback)
ISBN 978-1-7774547-5-3 (E-book)

To LG, VCM AND FRM

Extract from the Octopedia:

Over centuries, the Octopod home world had become less habitable as its seas shrank to fetid pools of salt. Elsewhere in the galaxy, Earth faced the opposite problem: an inexorable rise in water level drowning much of the land. An agreement was reached between the planetary governments to swap planets. Earth became Ocean, and the Octopod planet the new Earth.

Octopods had the better deal: they had long recognized that the rich plastic accumulations trapped in the great gyres—circulating currents of vast diameter on the ocean surface—provided an ideal environment for colonization. Plastic proved the perfect substrate for their pelagic civilization, plastic bottles in their trillions being an inexhaustible source of building material—infinitely malleable and coming in a wonderful palette of colours.

Chapter 1

THE WAVE OF anxiety made her vomit, which Devilly did discreetly into her mantle—that most practical part of the octopod anatomy. Had she stressed to Lawrence that he must cover the coral garden with plastic sheets, or her prize polyps would bleach in the sun? And would he remember to feed the rest of her menagerie? She had laid in a fortnight's stock of fry and left a note about Grunt. Her pet stonefish—the most venomous of its tribe—was a darling but could get peeved if not fed on time.

Lawrence Clutnife was on probation hired following the abrupt departure of the disgraced Henri. Finding a suitable replacement had been difficult. In reply to her request for a secretary-cum-butler, the agency had sent a skinny metamorph with literary pretensions and no clue about gardening. He was part-time, typing Devilly's manuscripts in the mornings and returning in the early evening to serve dinner. The afternoons he supposedly spent in rehearsal with a drama group: they had something "fringe" planned for an upcoming festival of theatre in Centro, the artistic hub of the Great Pacific Gyre. Erratic in his learning style, Lawrence alternated between obtuse about chores, and unnervingly swift when passing judgment on her writing.

The taxi to take her to the jetport arrived at an ungodly hour when the Gyre had barely turned towards the rising sun. She had packed at the last minute and was certain she had forgotten something vital—meds, passport, money. She sat hunched and miserable in the back, patting her various pouches anxiously. It was all Lawrence's fault.

Why? she asked herself for the umpteenth time. Why decide to go on holiday at all? She had work to do, but in truth her latest Daisy Cuttle mystery was not going well. Her fictional sleuth was stymied, the plot line hopelessly confused.

Mind you, on the upside, by going away she would miss Splashdown Day, the annual celebration of the first arrival of octopods on Earth. Devilly always felt that the planet swap arranged with the original inhabitants, a species of intelligent Arboreal, had been a sensible solution: worth celebrating, but not requiring—in Devilly's view—her presence. Better to watch it all on TV.

Although her village on an outer arm of the Great Pacific Gyre was small, Splashdown Day in Nether Vortex engaged most of the population. Organized—some might say marshaled—by Margo Seethe-Mantle from the manor house, the fete attracted octopods from across the sector to gawp at the parade. They would infest the gardens, snag any wild crab that might be so unwise as to venture across the open plastic, steal the bottles which weren't well cemented, and, worst of all, require a signed copy of Devilly's latest novel. Margo made a point of remarking how wonderful it was to have such a renowned writer resident in the village, and would she like the same table as before? Last year, Devilly had spent interminable hours under broiling plastic scrawling "Daisy Cuttle" hundreds of times until her signing tentacle bled. So where is Daisy? asked the disappointed punters, to which she explained to clear disbelief that Daisy Cuttle was a pen name.

And then there was the Parade, in which Devilly was supposed to sit on a float, pretending to write, under a swirling banner proclaiming Nether Vortex to be the abode of literary greats. Last year she had drifted behind a swim of polpitos and polpitas from the local school crooning a medley of the latest siren songs. It was not to be born.

So yes, when two weeks before, Lawrence had returned from retrieving the mail from the pool where letters in bottles swirled in common confusion—despite higher rates paid for so-called "express" delivery—Devilly had been vulnerable to suggestion.

Lawrence. Yes, he came with glowing testimonials. She had checked, of course: he had managed the country "cottage" of a family of Gyro aristocracy—the name vaguely familiar to Devilly. He had glowing reports from his last employer—something in underwriting—and he had graduated with a decent degree, albeit from one of the lesser schools.

Soon after his arrival, however, Lawrence stated that he wished to extend his skills as a registered metamorph in new directions. Metamorphs, a lesser caste of Octopod, were no longer content to be mere clotheshorses, subservient to their masters and mistresses; they needed to grow! He had tried—so he explained—impersonations of other molluscan species such as squid. All were unconvincing. By way of demonstration, he had manifested as a quasi-crab but even failed to stimulate Devilly's appetite for that species. He insisted that a sea slug was his go-to state, when he would resemble a gelatinous blob, something Devilly's guests would not want to see.

After some days of this lack-lustre shape-shifting, Lawrence announced that physical transformation was no longer his thing: henceforth he would practice different personalities and roles, these being less physically demanding and more rewarding spiritually. Consequently, during his trial as Devilly's secretary, he had morphed into literary agent, a part he now played with a languid glee.

A metamorph in the eternal quest for self, thought Devilly. Still, he could prove a useful foil, and help Devilly workshop some of her more complicated plots. But tending the anemone patch in her garden? No way.

"Now what?" she asked, sensing Lawrence's eagerness. He had returned at what was for him breakneck speed to hand her the post.

"You have an invitation!" Lawrence slid the bottle to within the grasp of Devilly's reading tentacle.

Devilly extracted a prospectus, lavishly illustrated with colourful octopods bathing in limpid waters, corals of every hue, and exotic reef-side restaurants.

"That's *Ripple*s by *Ochas Lagunas*," enthused Lawrence. "It is one of the finest of atoll resorts."

He had, of course, read the contents.

In a covering letter, she gathered she had won a free holiday to this resort. Her name had been picked at random, it seemed, by the company president. She vaguely remembered buying a raffle ticket at the last garden fête in Nether Vortex but had never bothered to look at the prizes.

"You think I should go on a package holiday?"

"*Ripples* is on the *Isla Florida*," replied Lawrence. "They promise exclusive access to your own lagoon, coral sands, and an unspoiled reef within a designated a Marine Protected Area. You can experience nature in the wild, it says."

"I never take a holiday abroad. The Gyre has all the attractions I need."

"Exactly! You've done the Gyre. You should get away from all this plastic. I've been reading the comments on your blog, and your fans share my opinion that your writing is getting stale. You need new experiences to nourish your muse."

Good Grief, thought Devilly, he is perfecting this agent role.

"But this *Ripples* is halfway across the ocean. I would have to fly. I don't like flying."

"As much food and drink as you like, and you have the choice of three sushi restaurants!"

"I would think so too. It is on a reef!"

"You can't turn down the opportunity," huffed Lawrence, fully launched into his role. "It's free and let's face it, you are blocked."

Chapter 2

S O FAR—AND IT was only 8 am—her day had been so nice she could kill. On arriving at the check-in counter two hours before takeoff, the scanner had rejected her QR code. She could sense impatience exude from the passengers jostling in the queue behind her. Flashing the pattern repeatedly, she had upped the saturation on her skin until the machine finally beeped acceptance. By which time her tentacle tips were bright red.

"And how will Madam be paying the extra charge for overweight baggage?" The RelaxJet agent behind the desk smiled sweetly.

Devilly sighed and waved the chip in her tentacle over the proffered machine. She watched her tagged bag float away to the nether regions, where she supposed it would be tossed about like a jellyfish in surf until loaded into the cargo sack of the RelaxJet charter.

Passing through security, she suffered the crowning indignity—the full body scan. Spread the tentacles please. How they could spot non-recyclable plastic, she had no idea. Then, on the far side, Security relieved her of her favourite slime, bought especially for her holiday and guaranteed to shield the skin from 99 percent of UV. There must be a circle of Hell reserved for these creatures.

"Have a nice day, Ma'am."

Breathing a deep draft of relief, Devilly jetted swiftly past shops guarded by bored sales squid, and exhibiting luxury items only affordable by the octopod super-rich. A finely tooled collier in rare plastic caught her eye, inlaid with black coral—ridiculously priced, though allegedly duty free.

From the periphery of her vision, she caught the sudden surge forward of a smart young octo flashing a logo on her flank advertising MerryVac.

"Excuse me, Ma'am. Are you fully insured for your flight today?"

"What's that?"

"For your flight. MerryVac travel insurance will ensure that you can enjoy the full travel experience. It takes seconds to sign up, and then no more worries about the expense of hospitalization . . ."

"No, no thank you, I already have insurance," said Devilly, trying to brush past.

". . . the policy includes a death benefit. No awkward health questions. Just a single payment today or spread it out over . . . peace of mind for the cost of a coffee day . . ."

Leaving peace of mind for the next victim, Devilly entered a tube leading to flight departures. She found herself behind a crowd of other passengers who seemed happy to drift forwards in the slow current. She jetted in short bursts to pass them. After what seemed like miles, the tunnel eventually broadened into a spacious cavern where the stillness and lack of movement contrasted with her recent dash through the importuning of duty-free commerce. At first, the departure pool seemed a haven of calm, painted a soothing teal and decorated with small artworks of some lesser-known bottle sculptors. But the calm was illusory; the waters tingled with tense expectancy. Hopeful passengers floated to and fro, glancing surreptitiously at the board to check for delays to boarding times. Families fidgeted; business types shuffled plastic memoranda in and out of their mantle portfolios.

The colourful display of magazines and books before one of the kiosks beckoned to Devilly. She was pleased to see one of her very own Daisy Cuttle mysteries on the bestsellers rack, albeit near the bottom. Very gratifying, but she had read it. The travel section held a small selection of guides to the various gyres, a Hitchhiker's Guide to the Shallows, but nothing on *Isla Florida*.

But why the phrase-books? It was a mystery to Devilly why Octo—a universally understood language—had, since arriving on Earth, mutated into different dialects. Perhaps it was the effect of place—the warm waters of the lower latitudes being conducive to romantic trills, whereas the harsher northern climes held hard to the pure Octo she had learned at school. Margo had suggested it might be wise to practice a little should she want to go shopping.

Devilly picked up a copy of Octo-Spanish that promised fluency in ten key phrases in only half an hour. Might as well, she thought, just in case the in-flight movie proved lousy.

Clutching her purchase with one sucker and her carry-ons with several of the others, Devilly looked for a quiet spot to settle down to await the call to board. A ledge overlooking the plastic bubble of the jetport would do. From here she could watch the languid movement and imagine the jocular raillery of the baggage handlers on the apron; the coupling and uncoupling of the food tanker; the departing cloud of cleaning shrimp hurrying to meet a new arrival of their next feast. Quite suddenly, all activity ceased. The crew on the apron disappeared from Devilly's view into the gloom beneath her overhanging bubble, leaving the wide-bodied jet to squat abandoned on its plastic mat. Tea-break, thought Devilly.

Not a bad idea. But would there be time? She looked around for a refreshment kiosk when . . .

"RelaxJet flight to *Isla Florida* boarding at Gate B."

The announcement barreled around the departure pool, echoing and rebounding, and causing the passengers to look enquiringly at each other. Is this the right one? Did you hear?

Yes, thought Devilly. Finally. She picked up her sack, already heavy with holiday reading to which she added the Octo-Spanish, her knitting, and a packet of crab snacks. She floated gently to the gate, waiting for the initial rush to subside. No issue with the QR here. A smile from the flight attendant, and she was aboard. These airline people are so professional and nice.

Devilly sank thankfully into the nook she had reserved so she could gaze at the waves. Molded in rigid plastic, the seating was a little loose for Devilly and there was far too little space for her longest arms behind the row in front. Oh well. Now she could relax, ready to discourage any conversation a fellow passenger beside her might venture, should ever one arrive. Boarding was almost completed. Roll on the headphones and a movie. Jetting was not something she enjoyed but it had its compensations.

But now, wafting down the aisle came her nemesis, an uncommonly large octopod clutching a panoply of those carry-ons that passengers are told to consign to the hold. Heather mixture patterns on its skin, an elderly male, with sagging folds and eye slits weeping oil. Please God no.

"You'll pardon me, Ma'am," said the newcomer, as Devilly knotted herself into a small ball. "I believe you are in my nook."

"What? Oh, I'm so sorry. I thought I had reserved the porthole. I'll move." So much for the view of the sea.

"No, no. Don't trouble yourself, dear lady. I really prefer being next to the cranny anyway. It lets one stretch the tentacles."

"Well, if you are sure . . ."

The large octopod squeezed into the nook beside Devilly, but even when settled, much of his corpulence bulged onto Devilly's side. She pulled herself a little tighter.

Movement! Devilly imagined the twin suck-jets at the rear of the craft inhaling seawater and squeezing it rearwards in narrow streams. They eased out of the Jetport and along the taxiway, platoons of bubbles spiraling towards the surface behind them.

They paused at the inner end of the strip of open water that led to the sea, the engines gulping in and pumping out in a low burble. The flight before them was waiting for a ground crew to make a final sweep of free-floating plastic, and to chase away with water cannon any careless gulls that might choke the jets.

From her window, Devilly watched the wide-bodied craft surge forwards. The Super-Albatross looked heavy, an inter-gyre route doubtless weighed down by business types, and impossibly heavier than air. It pushed out a broad wake, then the wings unfolded in a wide arc to cast a narrow shadow on the water. The speed gathered until, lifting reluctantly from the sea surface, it skimmed towards the open sea, turned and disappeared into the heat haze.

The steward came on the intercom to run through the safety procedures.

"The captain and crew welcome you to this RelaxJet flight. The safety card for this Albatross 320 is in the pouch in front of you. Please note that shortly we will be evacuating all water from the cabin, and the craft will rise above the surface. This is normal procedure prior to take-off. Should any passenger feel dehydrated during our flight, please pull the water mask from the pouch beside you and breathe deeply. Note that our water is filtered and purified. Now, please attach your seat suckers ready for take-off."

Slowly, the craft rose dripping above the surface and began to move. Devilly gripped fast to the walls of her nook while her neighbour scrabbled for the water mask.

"Sorry to be unsociable," he muttered, pulling the plastic hood over his siphon. "I will be fine once we get jetting."

The sudden acceleration thrust Devilly backwards. The throbbing of the suckjets rose in pitch. She looked out at plastic low-rise hangars beside the take-off lead streaming past the porthole, quicker and quicker. The craft rose on its step, and suddenly the main cabin lifted free of the clinging sea with only the trailing suckjets remaining below the surface, pumping furiously. They were *en route* to *Isla Florida*. Now, finally, Devilly felt she was on holiday.

Chapter 3

HER COMPANION WAS wriggling again, trying with his long reach to find something in the sack he had stuffed under the nook in front of him. With a gasp of effort, he pulled out a book. To Devilly's satisfaction, it was the pocket-plastic edition of her latest Daisy Cuttle mystery. She had noticed several copies on the sale rack at the shop in the departure pool. *Club Murder* was selling reasonably well, but her royalties had been tailing off recently.

From the corner of her slit pupil, she watched the man turn to the last chapter. Surely, if he just bought it for the flight, there had not been enough time for him to read from the beginning? One wonders why one bothers, thought Devilly, to develop characters and plot if the reader skips directly to the end. Perhaps a collection of short stories would sell, comprised entirely of the denouements of all her detective novels. She must mention the idea to her publisher.

Ten minutes later, her neighbour slapped the book shut.

"Damn good," he said, turning towards Devilly. "Have you read it? These detective mysteries are first class. Well-researched. She manages to keep us guessing too . . ."

He stopped, his gaze falling on the author picture on the back cover, then back to Devilly.

"You're not, you're not Devilly Peen, are you? Yes, you are! I'm good at faces."

"Er, yes."

"Wonderful. Let me introduce myself properly. My name is McKelpie . . ."

After some squirming, McKelpie managed to grasp one of Devilly's tentacles.

"Sandy McKelpie. Doctor, that was. Retired now, of course. I meant what I said: as a medical man, I really enjoy your novels. Your descriptions of death and injury are spot on. So many have no idea."

"You are very gracious. Very gratifying from a professional."

"Your Daisy Cuttle also seems to have some

inside knowledge of police procedures? I suppose you won't reveal your 'source'."

"Well, I have a nephew who is an inspector in Gyre Centro. He puts me straight on the details."

"Haha! I knew it. I don't suppose . . ." said McKelpie, reaching into his ink sac for a pen.

"Of course, of course."

Devilly signed the flyleaf with a flourish. This chap seemed harmless enough and since her neighbour was a doctor, even if retired, why waste the opportunity to seek some medical advice?

"I don't suppose," began Devilly adopting the same formula, "that you can recommend a good sun block. Mine was confiscated by security at the jetport. I hear that long exposure to the tropic sun can be fatal."

"You are right to be concerned. Octos underestimate the effects of exposure. I had a patient of mine once who came back from holiday a bright pink and stayed that way permanently. My advice is to remain underwater as much as possible, and if tempted above the surface, to slather yourself all over with slime. Look, let me write down a prescription."

McKelpie took out a small notebook and scribbled a couple of lines on a sheet. He tore it out and passed it to Devilly.

She tried to decipher the doctor's scrawl.

"I, er, can't quite read this bit."

"'Sunslime' is by prescription only. Fantastic stuff: it blocks 100% of UV and includes an antibiotic cream. Swear by it myself. Any chemist will know."

✦ ✦ ✦

"DRINKS, SNACKS, ANYTHING from the on-board menu?" The flight attendant was sliding towards them down the aisle.

"Let me buy you something," said McKelpie, signaling.

"No, I insist," he continued, waving away Devilly's objection. "What'll it be? A sachet of prosecco?"

"Oh, no alcohol, thank you. It will put me out," replied Devilly. "I'll just have tea."

The steward (he/she/it)—one could never really tell these days—was managing the awkward trolley with six of eight tentacles in a graceful ballet.

"And for you, sir?"

"A wee whiskey, with ice."

Brave man, thought Devilly. Drinking alcohol above water.

"Have you been to an *Ochas Lagunas* resort before?" asked McKelpie sucking his sachet of whiskey dry.

"No, this is my first time."

"Oh, I'm sure you will love *Ripples*. I have been to seven in all, one each year since my retirement. This will be number eight. Eighth and last. No idea what I'll do next year."

"Aren't they all the same?" asked Devilly.

"Oh, Lord no. *Ochas Lagunas* seeks out the best locations all over Ocean: on sea mounts, atolls, archipelagos. Now, let me see. There is *Deep Sea Wonderland*; and *Frosties* up in the high latitudes. The food is always local sourced, and they always have a variety of activities to feed the mind and body."

"Activities?" asked Devilly, suspicious. Having escaped Splashdown Day at home, she had no intention of being dragged into an *activity*.

"It's entirely up to you. Last place I was at, the events chappie was called Captain Funticle. He organized small group excursions. Splendid fellow; took us on some extraordinary dives. That was *Chockerlie* in the Scottish archipelago: a sea loch filled with plastic of the rarest pinks and purples. Quite beautiful in the evening with the sunsets filtering through. Of course, I would say that, being Scottish.

"You're from the North Atlantic Gyre, then?"

"Aye, the tips of the spiral brush the Scottish Isles, such as haven't been drowned by the rising seas."

"I had heard that the Atlantic Gyre had stopped spinning . . ."

"A rumour greatly exaggerated by the media. It still spins at a gentle pace, although I confess a complete revolution will be a long time coming."

"And yourself," continued McKelpie. "I read that you live in the Great Pacific Gyre. A bit too built up for my taste, I'm afraid. Nothing but row after row of bottle tenements."

"Oh, that's Centro. It's not all like that," replied Devilly. "My little village is quite rural, far out on one of the arms."

Conversation lapsed, and McKelpie was soon snoring beside her. Through the port, Devilly watched the tip of the wing beside her swoop up towards the sky as they crested the waves gathering momentum, before accelerating down into the troughs. Apparently, the swells were favourable today, which meant they only had to dip the suckjets below the surface occasionally to increase their speed. A good thing, thought Devilly, since she had read that the streaks of chum left across the surface by the churning of the jets was an environmental issue of concern. Flying in a flat calm was slow and problematic; but with these waves, they should arrive slightly ahead of time.

"This is your captain speaking. We are surfing along at six feet and will soon be arriving at *Isla Florida*. There may be a little turbulence as we settle back onto the water. Please ensure you are well seated in your nooks."

The cabin gave a sickening lurch.

"Six feet of altitude; seven foot wave," muttered her companion. "The inter-gyre flights travel at a smooth thirty, but I suppose these budget airlines have to skimp on fuel."

The Albatross settled onto the surface of the lagoon and sank, fresh seawater rushing into the cabin through the vents.

"That's a relief," said McKelpie. "I feel I can breathe again." He extricated himself from his nook and began amassing his various belongings. "I never check my sacks," he muttered to Devilly. "Travel light, my advice."

Through the port, Devilly watched the suction tube approach the cabin door, and moments later saw movement at the front of the cabin. She scrambled out behind McKelpie, to be washed down the aisle by the rush of passengers.

"Thank you for flying RelaxJet... have a great day..." called the steward, as they were sucked into the arrivals tube.

A long line of passengers waited at Immigration; no e-pass here, no biometrics scanner. There was impatience in the water; it had been a long day, and everyone resented this last hurdle before the beach. The single officer on duty looked harassed.

"*Appelido?* Name? Occupation? Purpose of visit?"

Only Devilly's occupation raised a flicker of interest.

"You that writer woman?"

"Yes."

"*Club Murder* great literature," he grunted, and brought down the stamp heavily on one of Devilly's tentacles.

"Enjoy your stay on *Isla Florida*. Maybe find mystery, yes?"

✧ ✧ ✧

"WE SHOULD SEE an octo waving a *Ripples* sign," called McKelpie, catching sight of Devilly looking lost in the concourse.

A mass of tentacles gesticulated from behind the barriers just outside the entrance. Each flashed an advertisement for a tour company, limousine, or hotel shuttle. It seemed total confusion.

"There!" cried McKelpie, taking her by the tentacle. He pointed to a large cuttlefish hanging in the water a little aside from the crowd. It held up a sign with a logo familiar to Devilly from the brochure—golden ripples beneath an azure sea.

"*Señores, benvenido*," lisped the cuttle, pulling the bags from their grasp and finning backwards rapidly. "We go to shuttle. *Ripples* very close. Is no distance."

The size of the lagoon surprised Devilly. From the brochure, she had imagined the atoll to be smaller and more intimate. Instead, they jetted past the coral gates to hotel resort after hotel resort, past new blocks of lagoon apartments stretching in rows of lookalike plastic. Every nook and cranny advertised bottle-grotte rentals. There was even a casino.

The shuttle driver pumped them along the inner side of the fringing reef, swerving to avoid an oncoming stream of jellyfish. "Crazy medusa!" yelled their driver over his shoulder.

Beside them ran a gleaming strip of coral sand. It was hot, the sun's rays burning through the very shallow water. Devilly glimpsed only a few octopods braving the sun. They lay sprawled on the sand, adopting various degrees of sun camouflage, some beneath the shade of shelters, hastily erected in a bright medley of coloured plastic sheets.

"Tide is out, I see. Aye, most of the tourists will be in the deeper pools," observed McKelpie.

Chapter 4

S ERAFIN FUNT SURVEYED his domain from
behind the reception desk with satisfaction.
In this interlude between the departure for the
jetport of one group of holidaymakers and the
arrival of the next, all was tranquil. Sunshine
filtering through the shallow waters of the
lagoon dappled the surface of the sand. The
shrimp had finished picking the crumbs from
the soft sponges in the lobby, and the outside
staff had realigned the ripples on the forecourt
to perfection.

Everything was in its place, polished and
waiting. His morning duties as Assistant Resort
Manager completed, Funt could relax. Breathing a deep draft of scented water, he adjusted
his skin colouration: today it was grey stripes
over a washed yellow—it spoke authority, he
judged, but with a hint of the Caribbean. Only a
few more minutes, perhaps, before the shuttle

bus arrived and disgorged its load of pallid and obese guests from the Gyre. He tried on his smile. Once in place, it would remain fixed for the full shift. He was also, for his sins, the resort's Director of Fun Activities. "Funt's the name, fun's the game", he reminded himself. Oh, Happy Day!

✧   ✧   ✧

THE *RIPPLES* RESORT by *Ochas Lagunas* occupies an isolated patch reef near one of the major channels leading from the lagoon through the main barrier to the ocean. It is prime real estate: a coral oasis rising above the floor of the shallow lagoon, surrounded by an apron of white sands stretching into the distant blue.

Giant urchins surrounded the entrance to the resort, their fearsome spines waving to warn off intruders. All were carefully tethered, Devilly noticed, as their driver whisked them through a gap in the prickly fence and up to reception.

"Never know what to tip these people,"

muttered Sandy McKelpie to Devllly. He fumbled inside his mantle and extracted a few cowries for their hovering driver who smirked a *gracias* and backed swiftly away.

The resort's lobby was a cavern carved into the living coral. Devilly spotted a species which she had tried to cultivate in her garden back in Nether Vortex. Here it grew in a resplendent arch above the reception desk, its polyps extended in purple profusion.

A pair of squid approached to drape weed around the new arrivals, supervised by a smiling octopod in the faded colours of tropical linen. The octo—a male with a slightly seedy air in Devilly's lightening judgment—turned towards her and her companion, and for the briefest moment turned even paler, matching the colour of the coral sand on the floor of the cavern. Reverting quickly, he slithered towards Devilly, tentacles outstretched in greeting.

"Welcome, welcome to *Ripples*, Madam," he said, ignoring McKelpie. "I trust your journey has not been too awful." He turned to one of the squids and flicked a tentacle towards her bags.

"Let me introduce myself. Serafin Funt, at your service. I am the Assistant Resort Manager. If there is anything you need, please don't hesitate to let me or any of the squid know. At *Ripples*, your happiness is our business."

Funt withdrew behind the counter as Devilly turned to follow her bags.

"Well, this is where we must part company, I'm afraid," said McKelpie. Both had received bands for their tentacles. Devilly's was a bright yellow; McKelpie's a dull brown.

"Oh, why? Are we not in the same place?"

"You have a yellow band. It seems us browns are over on the far side overlooking the sea-grass meadow; yellows are nearer the channel." For a moment, McKelpie looked thoughtful. "Odd that, but I am sure I've seen that chap Funt before at one of the other resorts. I suppose they move them around; don't you think?"

McKelpie hovered closer and touched Devilly's tentacle again.

"Goodbye for now. I expect we shall meet again at dinner. Give me time to finish that story I was telling you on the flight."

Don't count on it, thought Devilly. With a choice of three restaurants and a cafeteria in the resort, it should be possible to avoid Sandy McKelpie.

◇　◇　◇

DEVILLY WAS PLEASED to discover that her assigned grotte was indeed on the side of the patch reef closest to the channel. From the balcony, she could look out to where the edge of the deeper water was marked by the waving fronds of a line of fan corals. The tide had turned, and the current surging into the lagoon would be carrying—so she hoped—an assortment of snacks from beyond the reef. Soon, the influx of water would deepen the lagoon, and it would be sufficiently cool to venture out to find one of those restaurants for something substantial to eat. Her appetite had quite returned; she had already noted that *The Rip Tide* offered soft-shelled crab *à la volonté*.

Chapter 5

To her disappointment, Devilly's first choice of restaurants required a reservation, forcing her to eat at Salty's Poolside Cafeteria from a self-serve buffet. The food, however, had been alive and exotic—all deliciously tropical—and very different from her normal supper on a tray back home in Nether Vortex. She couldn't try all the dishes, but she made a start. Washed down with a couple—or was it three?—of Salty's famous punch, she had floated back to her grotte in a warm current, guided by slivers of pale light from a globular moon that bulged and wavered on the sea surface. It had been a full day, and Devilly looked forward to a solid night's sleep.

She awoke a couple of hours later with an uneasiness in her crop and spent much of the remaining night hovering between bed and bathroom. What, she wondered, had possessed her to experiment with the sashimi medley. It had contained the most colourful fish—presumably freshly caught—and she had gorged herself, forgetting that first rule of a foreign vacation: to approach meals with caution. To Devilly's distress, much of the medley revisited her overnight.

Considering herself a serious student of marine life, Devilly had bought with her a handy plasticized guide to the reef fish of *Isla Florida*. Now in the pale light of dawn, lying weakly on her bed, she made a mental note to carry it with her whenever she went out to dine.

This won't do, said Devilly to herself. Pull yourself together. You are on holiday!

Floating uncertainly to the edge of her grotte, she opened the plastic blinds. Outside, rays of bright sunshine slanted down through the water, reflecting harshly from the white coral sand. Ouch! She gathered herself, focusing on pumping melanin into her eye filters before venturing out.

Finding her way back to reception proved more difficult in daytime than at night—the water was hot, and she had to dodge from one shadowed pool to the next under the overhang of the reef. A squid marshaling a bevy of cleaning shrimp pointed her in the right direction and, after a few minutes, she jetted thankfully into the dim of the cavernous lobby.

A crowd of octopods was hanging in the water, surrounded by a jetsam of sacks and clutches; an outbound group of tourists, she supposed, waiting for their transfer to the jetport. She jetted towards the reception desk on a mission sure that they must have something for upset stomachs. Indigestion from eating raw reef food must be a common complaint. As she approached, she noticed a pair of uniformed officers to one side, discreetly flashing their blue and white. They seemed to be studying a list provided by the clerk from behind the counter. Police. Well, her needs were more urgent.

"Ahem!"

The three octos turned towards Devilly. The clerk, she noticed, looked a particularly obsequious shade of puce.

"If you wouldn't mind waiting . . ." began the clerk.

"No, no. Please serve the Señora." The longer of the two octopods extended a greeting tentacle to Devilly and surveyed her with a professional eye. "Sergeant Caracol and I are merely doing our routine check of new arrivals. Might we know your name and where you are visiting us from, Señora?"

"I, er. Devilly Peen. From Nether Vortex on the Great Pacific Gyre."

The officer blinked his slit eyes.

"Not the author of the Daisy Cuttle mysteries, surely? But yes, of course you are. *Madonna!* This is such an honour. I am Comandante Pesquero. You are most welcome to *Isla Florida.*"

"You," he said turning to the clerk. "Assist the Señora immediately."

"I must apologize, Señora Peen. Our island ways must seem slow compared with the Gyre."

"Not at all. I only arrived last night, and everyone has been very helpful."

"*Excelente!* Caracol, do you still have that book by the Señora?"

The corporal pulled a battered copy of

Eight for Dinner in Spanish translation from his mantle. It had last been reprinted five years previously, and it was obvious that this volume had passed between many a sucker.

"It would do me a great favour, Señora, to have your autograph."

"Well, of course, Comandante, "replied Devilly, taking the book. "To whom should I dedicate it?"

"To '*Pepita*', Señora. Et *gracias*. Perhaps we will meet again. Until then, I wish you a most pleasant stay."

Gosh, thought Devilly, he actually clicked his heels. She watched the two officers swim back through the entrance of the cavern and disappear into the bright blue void. She turned back to the reception clerk and stopped short. For the life of her, she couldn't remember what she had come down for.

Chapter 6

B Y LATE MORNING, Devilly was still lying in her nook with the blinds drawn. This was no way to spend a holiday, she decided, not while the reef beckoned. Now feeling a little peckish, she resolved to venture out to find the crab shack pictured in the orientation guide she had picked up in the lobby.

The rays of the brilliant noontime sun bore through the water, warming her back as Devilly scudded across the sand following the signs to the shack. It turned out to be easy to find, a snack bar fashioned from a giant clam shell, nestling in the shelter of a fan coral. This was more like it. She ordered a crustacean smoothie and retreated to one of the alcoves that overlooked the coral garden. The lawns of rippled sand ended abruptly at the dim wall of the main reef. It seemed tantalizingly close, but signs warned of a strong current.

Feeling restored, she decided to explore the gardens around the resort.

"Lady needs a parasol?" A rather disheveled squid had materialized in front of her alcove. It was clutching a large bundle of rolled sunshades. Well, it was rather hot. Devilly parted with a couple of cowries for a sheet of opaque plastic in cheerful orange and green stripes.

"*¡Oí! ¡Vete! ¡Escoria!*" Devilly looked to see who was calling. One of the resort security squids was approaching, flashing red. When she swiveled again to look for her vendor, it had disappeared: only the puff of disturbed sand suggested it was ever present.

"I am so sorry, Señora. The resort does not allow those scum on the grounds."

"Oh. Well, thank you. I hadn't realized."

"Is not permitted to feed the squid. *¡Está prohibido!*"

"I see."

"*Buenas tardes*, Señora."

A little unnerved by this encounter, Devilly, after draining her drink, decided to swim a circuit around the patch reef while staying safely within the boundaries of the resort. After

the security guard had jetted away, she unfolded her new parasol and set off in the opposite
direction.

Ripples was certainly very pretty in a mani-
cured sort of way—the sea grass on lagoon-
side raked into regimental order, the brain
corals in perfect spheres. A parrot fish tended
to a thicket of staghorn coral, nibbling the
stalks to a pleasingly uniform height. Devilly
glimpsed a crew discreetly removing an antler
tumbled by the current, but she encountered
little other signs of life. Where were all the
guests?

She followed an arrow indicating the way to
Pirate's Lookout, advertised as the highest
point of the resort. On the way up, she met
someone coming down—a harassed looking
octo father dragging two young polpitos by
their tentacles.

"It is much too hot up there. You will boil,"
he muttered, hurrying past.

True enough, the water slopping across the
partially exposed reef top was sauna tempera-
ture, and despite her parasol, Devilly did not
want to linger. However, having made the

effort, she would have a quick look around. Letting herself bob to the surface, she lassoed a nearby coral head that rose just above the water and clambered onto it. She let her eyes adjust to the open air. Seaward, a line of spray marked where waves were breaking on the outer barrier reef. Suddenly, a column of water erupted, a fountain rising high into the air. Could it be, thought Devilly, the spouting of some giant whale? Even from this distance, it was an impressive sight.

The onshore breeze drying her eyes, Devilly turned her back to the wind. Inshore, in contrast to the turmoil on the reef, all was tranquil. As if painted on canvas, a yellow line marked the beach at the edge of the lagoon, backed by a low green wall. Further still, shrouded in haze, a grey cone rose skywards. *Isla Florida*, she recalled from the guidebook, was actively volcanic.

Enough! Devilly let herself sink below the surface, and she jetted quickly down the path into the deeper water of the lagoon. Continuing around the grounds, she drifted over a shell garden—immaculately sorted according to size—and soon found herself back in front of the lobby, having completed her circumnavigation of the resort.

Inside, currents of cooler water were swirling across the floor of the cavern from the climate control fans, and several groups of octopods were lounging about. To one side of the lobby, a colourful display of assorted brochures caught her eye.

"Ah, Ms. Peen?"

She recognized the voice of Serafin Funt, the Assistant Manager and Director of Fun Activities, whom she had met on arrival. Today, he was sporting the blue and yellow blazer of the resort, and beside him a pair of local squid grinned a welcome.

"You have come to sign up for some of our activities and excursions? Wonderful. Wonderful."

"I, er . . ."

"Private tours of the reef front, for the adventurous. Dive deep to see the purple corals. Or you might prefer something more cultural. We do a tour of the Old Quarter of the lagoon: a half day with reduced admission to historical sites, and with a chance to sample authentic local cuisine!"

"But I have just . . ."

"Exotic wildlife! That's your thing, I'm sure. See the parade of land crab on a land-side safari. Led by an experienced local guide, and secure within the resort's bubblebus."

Devilly was susceptible. Her circuit of the gardens was pleasant enough, but frankly a little tame. And why was she here if not for new experiences. It was all grist to the writer's mill. Perhaps the Old Quarter would provide material.

"Well, perhaps the cultural tour . . ."

"Excellent. Excellent. We have a small group leaving at two o'clock this afternoon, and you have the last space. Unfortunately, the later tours are booked solid. So perhaps I can add your name?"

"Yes, all right. I'll take it." Devilly passed her tentacle with its credit insert over the proffered machine.

"Good, Good. Two sharp, here in the lobby. Thank you, Madam." Funt gave her a brilliant smile and turned away as he caught sight of the father with offspring Devilly had met previous-ly.

"*¡Hola!* Señor! Funt's the name and fun's the game. The resort is offering a treasure hunt on the inner reef this afternoon. A private guide and full supervision for the young'uns. An experience of a lifetime for your handsome polpitos. Only . . ."

Devilly drifted away out of earshot towards the rear of the lobby. She had no doubt that Funt would sign up another victim. Still, a cultural tour sounded educational, catering to adult tastes, and intellectually stimulating. Perhaps she might meet someone interesting. Well, someone anyway: Devilly had become a little bored being alone, and even beginning to miss Lawrence's pretentious chatter back home.

✧　✧　✧

FIVE MINUTES BEFORE 2 pm, Devilly was waiting in the lobby, looking around for her tour leader. There was no sign of Serafin Funt, but an elderly threesome floated nearby in a gentle eddy. She approached in her blandest colouration and coughed.

"Excuse me, are you with the Culture Tour?"

"Why, yes, we are. We are just waiting for Mr. Funt. Are you joining us? That will make four."

"I thought the tour was going to be with a larger group. I was told they had no more space."

"Oh, everyone here is out to sell you something. Blenny bought a coral bracelet yesterday, and it turned out to be plastic. What can you do? We are the Musselshucks from Brooklyn, Lem and Blenny. Over there is Carlton, our best third. We never go anywhere without him."

"Devilly."

They touched tentacles. The Brooklyn sector that Devilly remembered from her student days had been low rent and carefree. But that part of Gyre Centro had since gentrified: rents had sky-rocketed and most of the old brown plastic tenements torn down to be replaced by lofts and coffee shops. Still, the Musselshucks seemed genuine enough; Lem certainly had the accent she remembered.

"Is Carlton your?"

"Yes, still hanging around after all these years. We are a proud triple. Not so common these days."

True, thought Devilly. Octopod biology required three to reproduce—triploid vigour was taught early in sex education—but these days threesomes didn't seem to last. Even in her backwater of Nether Vortex, she knew of several singles and doubles. Times change.

"The polps have swum away, of course," Blenny interrupted. "We have one still living in Centro helping Lem with the shop. Lemi Junior moved to Perrier—he is in banking—and our youngest, Concha, has gone to university. She is going to be a lawyer!"

"How nice," replied Devilly. "Ah! Here comes our guide, I think . . ."

Funt hurried up to them, accompanied by a rather sullen looking young octopod.

"I am so, so sorry. Last minute thing came up. But here we are!"

"We've been waiting here for . . ." began Devilly.

"Ah, the Musselshucks, and Ms. Peen, delighted. Of course, of course. You must all be anxious to set off! Now, our tour this afternoon starts just outside the lobby here. There will be three more joining us, I believe. Ah! Here are the Crabbles, and, er, it says 'Yogpot' on my list."

The arriving Crabbles were flushed and pumping furiously.

"The service in these restaurants is extremely slow," said the largest of the new arrivals. "My name is Crabble, by the way." He paused to regain his breath and survey the assembly. "And this is Mrs. Crabble, and our son Precious. 'Yogpot', eh? I'm afraid Mrs. Crabble does indulge him."

Oh God, thought Devilly at the thought of spending the afternoon in the company of Yogpot. What was he, twelve? Her thought of escaping back to her room was interrupted by Funt.

"I see the bubblebus is just pulling up. Just a quick word about your itinerary. From here, you will travel along the inner edge of the barrier—watch out for the plentiful marine life—all the way to the eastern end of the lagoon where the first octopods settled on *Isla Florida* only a few years after Splashdown. They made their home in the Old Quarter—the *Casco Antiguo*, as they say. If, like me, you are intrigued by architecture, some of the bottle-grottes date back to that period: the kitsch influence is quite pronounced. We do provide a lunch, but you must try some of the special seafood from our local vendors. You will taste nothing fresher than the Top of the Tide, I assure you. Afterwards, you will have a couple of free hours to wander around absorbing the atmosphere, and for the ladies to do a spot of shopping, haha."

"I was looking at the map, Mr. Funt, and I couldn't find anywhere around the lagoon called the Old Quarter. Where would that be exactly?" asked Devilly.

"Eh?" Funt came over and looked at the map of the island spread between Devilly's tentacles. "Oh, I see. Some of these tourist maps are not very detailed." He flicked a tentacle at the map. "There. Some refer to it as "Tire Town". It's a rather droll name, I know—

a touch of local colour!"

"Will there be a stop for the facilities, Mr. Funt," enquired Blenny Mussselshuck, anxiously.

"Of course, of course. Now, I think we should mount up. The tide waits for no octo, as they say."

Devilly trailed Funt and the group out of the lobby to their waiting transport.

"This is where I leave you, I'm afraid," announced Funt at the door to the bubblebus. "Let me introduce Ernesto, your driver—Ernesto muttered something incomprehensible in response—and Pleća Kalamarnica here will be your guide this afternoon."

He gestured to the octo trailing behind him.

"Don't be shy about asking questions. Pleća will surely have the answer. Say 'hello', Pleća!"

Pleća Kalamarnica's scowl—which she had been wearing for the last ten minutes, cracked into a grudging smirk as her mantle turned a pinkish purple, causing the simulated tattoos which she had been flashing to merge into her general colour scheme.

"Sure, Hi. I have degree in Arboreal Archaeology and History of Plastic Architecture. Now I work as tour guide."

"Yes, well," said Funt, hurriedly. "All aboard? Enjoy your afternoon!"

Chapter 7

NOBODY SPOKE AS the bus jetted along the reef edge. Most of the passengers—except the junior Crabble whose eyes remained locked on his tablet—gazed through the transparent bodywork of the bubblebus at the passing kaleidoscope of colours: corals of differing hues, anemones in scarlet and orange, blue sea squirts, silver barnacles; the flash of reef fish veering from their path. Looking through the plastic floor, Devilly spotted a lobster scrambling for shelter as their shadow flitted over it. However, there would be no stopping for closer examination.

Gradually, however, the diversity of marine life declined. Devilly guessed that they must have crossed from the Marine Protected Area into waters which were intensively fished. What species remained were skittish, quick to burrow in the sand or flee at top speed.

"Now we get near Tire Town," called Pleća Kalamarnica, suddenly. "When bus stops, we go outside. Hold on to wallet."

They halted in the shade of an overhanging coral that had grown in a ring-like form that Devilly had not seen before. Pleća Kalimarnica ensured they were all together and then led off into a tangle of weed that screened a murky wall of coral rising from the otherwise feature-less floor of the lagoon. Swimming through a maze of passages and tunnels, they passed rounded shapes stacked one on top of each other. Although black beneath, pale pink algae encrusted their sides and tops. The unusual formation piqued Devilly's curiosity. Where one had tumbled to the lagoon floor, Devilly saw that it was hollow, the interior encircled by a dark cavern from which she glimpsed the spines of some unknown occupant. Devilly was about to ask a question when their guide halted the group.

"Tires," she announced, anticipating Devilly and pointing to one of the round shapes. "Is why they call it Tire Town. Now I tell history. Before Splashdown, many revolutions, *Isla*

Florida was much bigger, joined to drowned continent. Many arboreals lived here. This is important archaeological site of the Anthropocene epoch."

"But hey," demanded Lem Musselshuck. "What's with these 'tires', and why so many of them here?"

"Is hypothesis that were thrown to sea gods to stop sea level rising. Analysis shows they are made of rubber, a substance grown on trees and very expensive. So maybe rings to fit fingers of gods. Giant squid perhaps."

"But . . ." began Devilly.

"Can't argue with Science," said Musselshuck.

"We must move on now to reach Old Quarter," insisted Pleća.

They jetted slowly after their leader. Once, as they neared a particularly large and dark recess, their guide stopped abruptly.

"Big hole. Giant moray eel. Maybe take other way."

Through a jumble of smaller tires, though crannies and twisting alleys, the group streamed along—perhaps a little warier of the blacker cavities—before arriving in an open arena of coral sand.

"Old Quarter town square," announced Pleća. "We go to monument." She led the way, finning swiftly across the bare sand to where a single giant tractor tire rose from the seafloor, balanced on its edge.

"But it's round," objected the junior Crabble. "Why do they call it a square?"

Too engrossed to pay much attention to Pleća's response, Devilly was reading the plaque at the base of the monument.

Erected some few revolutions after Splashdown, it commemorated the first colonizers—adventurers really—who were scouring the oceans for sources of quality plastic. They were disappointed: all they discovered on *Isla Florida* were tires. Reinforced with steel and too heavy to float, they proved of no use for open-water construction. Never wealthy, the small founding colony of octopods persisted, finding that tires *in situ* provided adequate shelter, and on the nearby reef could be hunted an abundance of food. They had learned by trial and error whether an unfamiliar species was edible or toxic. Martyrs to their curiosity, read the inscription.

By now it was late afternoon, and as the sun rays filtered obliquely through the waters of the shallow lagoon, the Old Quarter stirred in the cooler shade. Vendors began setting out their wares, and bars and restaurants spilled out onto the sand from crevices in the wall of tires.

"Free time now," called their guide. "For shopping. We meet here at monument in two hours." Pleća Kalamarnica jetted off abruptly to the far side of the square and disappeared.

The Musselshucks looked at the Crabbles and the Crabbles looked at the Musselshucks. Everyone looked at Devilly.

"Well," said Devilly after a pause and pointing after the departing guide. "I think the shops are mostly that way ..."

"Oh Lemi, Carlton, just look at those colours." Blenny was already pulling her cohort towards a stall on the north side of the square, where brilliant flags waved invitingly in the current. The Crabbles moved to follow.

"I wanna ..."

Before she discovered the cravings of the

Yogpot, Devilly excused herself to explore alone. She did not approve of the modern trend for parents to keep their larvae close. In Devilly's view, young people needed a planktonic phase to learn about life. Young Crabble needed a dose of natural selection.

A tottering stack of tires walled the square on its south side. The tires seemed to reach almost to the surface. Devilly let herself rise slowly upwards, peering into little recesses and hollows. Her passing shadow caused decorative anemones on the balconies to retract their arms abruptly, guard clams to snap closed. She felt multiple eyes watching her. From some holes, tentacles waved invitingly. While the Old Quarter had first seemed an easy-going and bohemian place, increasingly she felt a vague menace. As a tourist, she was prey.

The top tier of the Old Quarter was awash with the slight swell that eased over the reef into the lagoon. Back home on the Gyre, thought Devilly, such a penthouse view would command an exorbitant rent; here the rooftops looked insalubrious, covered with green algal slime. From just below the surface, she got a better sense of Tire Town as it sloped away into the gloom of the deeper water. It seemed a monotonous prospect of tumbled rubber with only the occasional bleached coral head providing any relief. Suddenly, a cloud cast a deep shadow, and a breeze sent a battalion of ripples across the sea surface. Devilly felt a sudden chill. She took a last look before descending again, and it suddenly struck her: there were no fish. Only far off in the murk did long shadows hang motionless in mid water. She didn't care to speculate what they might be.

Sinking back to the bottom, Devilly alighted at the entrance to a broad canyon winding into the wall of tires. Here there seemed to be more bustle, and she saw octos of various stripes going about their business. Relieved, she followed this thoroughfare for a few minutes. As she ventured further, it became less obviously touristic, the stalls catering to the needs of the locals.

A large sign for "Monsieur Le Pieuff's Emporium and Poison Palace" caught her eye. An arrow pointed towards a shadowy crevasse in the wall of tires. Dollar store? Pharmacy? Devilly was curious and drifted closer to examine the display in the window: variously coloured sachets whose contents were reputed to have aphrodisiac properties; good luck seahorses tethered by their tails and looking mournful; starfish pinned to the ceiling in astrological patterns. There were self-help books, and plenty of nacre for self-reflection. Strings of coral beads draped over the entrance. A handwritten notice stated that prescriptions filled for a happy life. She was about to turn away when . . .

"Lady needs a leetle potion for this evening? Something to tingle desire?"

"Well, no. I think I'll just . . ."

"Only poison shop in the lagoon. Lady will find anything she needs."

A pallid octo emerged from the shadows, thin tentacles reaching to draw Devilly in. It was a half-caste, she judged: half octo, half squid. She reprimanded herself for her unconscious specism.

"We have cures for all sickness; lagoon has nasty stingers. Please, please come inside to see."

By way of research, thought Devilly. One of her hobbies was collecting samples of poisons from venomous sea creatures. Back home in Nether Vortex, she had quite a reputation for her knowledge, and had even assisted the Gyre police in suspicious cases. Now, she always carried in her poison sac a selection of the commoner venoms and their antidotes. One never knew when she might need them. As to entering the Poison Palace, what was the harm? She didn't have to buy anything.

"I would be interested in seeing your local cone shells."

"*Si*, Lady. Of these poisonous snails, we have a great variety. Please, this way."

She allowed the octo to usher her into the shop, which she had assumed would be a shallow grotto. But, as her eyes adjusted to the gloom, she saw it enlarged into a cave extending far to the rear. Bioluminescent polyps dangling from the roof provided dim illumination. Along one wall, plastic partitions separated several of the fierce molluscs. She recognized the commoner species, but there were one or two completely new to Devilly. It must have been soon after feeding time: impaled on the spears of the cones were several small fish in various stages of digestion.

"And you have all the antidotes?" she asked, lingering over a specimen checkered in black and white: *Conus litteratus*, the Alphabet Cone. She had one at home that she hoped Lawrence was feeding regularly.

"Lady, it is the regulation."

"And those jellyfish," said Devilly, pointing to long streamers tethered to the far wall. "Have you extracts of the siphonophore nematocysts?" She was only too familiar with the agonizing sting of the Portuguese-Man-of-War.

"Lady, I am only minding the store." The octo waved its tentacles and flashed colours of despair. "Monsieur Le Pieuff will be back soon. He can answer all your questions."

Devilly drifted across to look in a display cabinet.

"I will take these," she said, pointing to a pair of small starfish. She felt sorry for the student and thought the small gift might go well with Pleća Kalamarnica's piercings.

Then another thought occurred to Devilly.

"Do you make up prescriptions? I have this for a sunblock." She fished in her mantle and showed the paper McKelpie had given her. The octo scrutinized the writing, then nodded.

"Of course. We have all these ingredients." He scurried behind the curtain at the end of the cavern, leaving Devilly to further inspect the unusual offerings of the emporium. He returned a minute later.

"Must apply twenty minutes before exposure," insisted the octo. "Very high test, very good. Is ten clams."

"Do you accept plastic?"

"*Si*, Lady."

There was a sudden commotion at the entrance to the cavern.

"Ah, here is Monsieur Le Pieuff. He will be delighted to meet such a beautiful lady with so many questions." The shop assistant's voice tailed off as they both heard a loud exclamation from outside.

"*Espece d'ordure! Los Picos* will hear of this . . . I pay for protection." A shadow blocked most of the light from outside as the new arrival turned to enter the shop. On seeing Devilly, he stopped short mid-water. His colour made a lightning change from a furious scarlet to a soothing green.

"Ah, *Madame*, a thousand pardons. I am accosted by this, this ordure outside. You must not alarm yourself; I have, how you say, seen it off. Serge Le Pieuff, at your command."

"Devilly Peen."

"*Enchanté*, Madame. I trust my assistant here has been of service, even if he knows nothing, the cretin."

"Oh, yes. He has been very helpful. But I was wondering whether you stock any of the rarer venom. I have a modest collection myself on the Gyre, but here I imagine here you find species of marine life unknown in mid-ocean."

"And these substances, would *Madame* have a specific purpose in mind?"

"Oh, I was thinking something that might have an amusing effect. For a party trick, for instance. Naturally one would want to have the antidote as well."

"*Madame* refers to certain jellyfish whose sting creates amusing convulsions? I have a selection, and they come with a soothing balm.”

“Hm. For my research only, I was wondering if you can recommend anything stronger?”

Le Pieuff glanced a little nervously towards the blue curtain drawn across the rear of the cavern. When he spoke again, it was in a low confidential tone.

“*Madame* makes a joke?”

“No. You see, I am interested because of the books I write. They are mostly murder mysteries ... so do you stock extract of blue-ring octopus, something from the phyllidia nudibranchs, or Chironex—the box jellies?”

Monsieur Le Pieuff grew serious, regarding Devilly with new respect.

“It might be possible to acquire such items, but *Madame* should be aware that there may be difficulties with customs.”

Devilly looked at the time. Her two hours were nearly up. It was time to go.

“This has been most interesting, Monsieur Le Pieuff. Now I must hurry back to the plaza.”

“If *Madame* would care for our special catalog?” said Le Pieuff as Devilly was backing towards the street. "It is for our most discerning customers, for whom we can always arrange delivery."

✧ ✧ ✧

ALTHOUGH DEVILLY WAS only a few minutes late, Pleća Kalamarnica was floating at the door of the bubblebus, flashing an impatient red.

"Is time to leave! We wait for you."

"I am so sorry . . . there is so much to see . . . I thought you might like these."

"Oh," said Pleća, taken aback. "That is most kind. I have kept snack for you from Turn of the Tide restaurant." She rummaged in her mantle and pulled out a six-inch wrap.

"I think is shrimp inside."

Devilly was touched. She was sure their guide had hoped to keep this for her supper. She fingered the mysterious cling-wrapped snack.

"No, you keep this. I ate in the Old Quarter."

Climbing inside, Devilly found the Musselshucks sprawled across their seats, Lem and Carleton fast asleep; Blenny, clutching in her tentacles an assortment of purchases glared at her, and then averted her gaze. The Junior Crabble sat at the rear of the bus, his parents on either side as if transporting a delinquent—silent but both the colour of a stormy sunset.

The driver seemed to take a more direct return route to the resort; they were further away from the barrier reef and crossed mostly featureless sand. Only an occasional puff of sand showed where some well camouflaged denizen scooted away from their path. On their left, a desolate waste of broken coral stretched away inshore. Their guide—mollified by the charm Devilly had bought her as a gift—saw the direction she was looking.

"Is the *barrio*. Very poor. Much crime, drugs. Young people leave. Want to go to Gyre for better life."

"That's sad," replied Devilly. "And this is such a beautiful lagoon. What about you, Pleća?"

"Yes. I go after season over. Back to school."

"You are still studying?"

"Oh, yes. Must finish thesis on Arboreal Ritual Sites. But grant money very small. Is why

I work for Señor Funt."

"How fascinating," said Devilly. "I suppose your sites are few and far between on the Gyre; being in mid-ocean, it must be hard to find a site to dig."

"Not so. In floating garbage, we find many artifacts. In my thesis, I reconstruct Arboreal village from their discarded plastic."

"Mostly made of bottles, I suppose. I've often wondered if they lived like us in Nether Vortex."

By the time they were approaching the gates of *Ripples*, Devilly had learned much about how the study of microplastics could date artifacts; how using sophisticated techniques, science could build a picture of the life of an average arboreal. All their civilization rendered down to a collection of plastic beads; how sad, she thought.

Chapter 8

THE BUBBLEBUS DEFLATED with a long hiss. Devilly was the last to be ejected. She thanked Pleća and the driver with appropriate clams, and then followed the Musselshucks and the Crabbles into the lobby.

"Bed for us," announced Lem Musselshuck and Carleton simultaneously, while supporting a wilting Blenny between them. The Crabbles had already disappeared. Left hovering alone in the middle of the lobby, feeling tired but accomplished, Devilly needed refreshment. The café/bar to one side of Reception looked promising.

The Sea Fan strove for sophistication but settled for tropical kitsch. The furnishings were plush sponges in pastel shades, with encrustations from the same palette. Eponymous fans beckoned discreetly over several inviting alcoves, and framed posters from other resorts by *Ochas Lagunas* decorated the walls.

A lone octo propped up one end of the bar. There was something about him that caught her eye: his green, yellow, and purple skin pattern almost matched the coloured bottles arrayed on a shelf behind the counter. Deliberate camouflage thought Devilly fleetingly, but then garish dress seemed the norm among the holidaymakers.

She spotted a quiet corner and settled down to look at the bar menu. Tucked below the list of exotic cocktails, she found a selection of small plates on offer. She was tempted, but should she risk raw again? Tea seemed absent from the list.

A familiar voice interrupted her deliberations.

"Ah, what a delightful coincidence, Ms. Peen. I was hoping our paths would cross again."

Damn it, thought Devilly: Sandy McKelpie. Normally her antennae worked well, but it had been a long afternoon.

"Let me buy you that drink. You cannot refuse this time; we are safely underwater."

McKelpie slumped into the seat beside her. Not his first of the day, it seemed.

"Chance to finish that story I was telling you on the flight over," he said, signaling the barkeep with a florid tentacle.

"Punch for this famous lady," he bellowed. "And another for me."

Devilly was embarrassed. Fortunately, the lounge was still empty except for the octo at the bar who seemed oblivious to McKelpie's shouted order.

Trapped. Ten minutes later, McKelpie was still describing the pleasures of the seven *Ochas Lagunas* resorts that Devilly really must visit. So much so that she began to feel that *Ripples* barely scraped three stars compared with the others.

"Mind you," McKelpie continued. "There was an unpleasant business last time. Chap died in a nasty accident on one of the excursions. Some suspected it might be a murder. Still, that shouldn't put *you* off!"

"And tomorrow, dear lady, allow me to escort you. I have booked a tour of the resort's reef. They promise a view of the marvelous biodiversity; we may even see a shark! You must put a shark into your next Daisy Cuttle mystery."

God, these amateurs! They really have no idea of the creative process. Devilly gently removed a straying appendage.

"Well, I..." At that moment, Devilly glimpsed Funt crossing the lobby, trailed by a stream of new arrivals. "...I'm afraid I have already signed up for something tomorrow. That is such a pity."

McKelpie looked crestfallen. "But we must have dinner tomorrow night after you return. Perhaps we can meet again here?"

Devilly rose, and—a little hastily—jetted towards the lobby. As she passed the bar, she noticed that its lone customer had left; only the barkeep remained, vaguely wiping a glass. He smirked at Devilly.

"*Buenas noches*, Señora."

Chapter 9

IT WAS TO be surfing at Silver Sands, an "activity" designed to amuse the younger generation of octopods. When Devilly had, in desperation, approached Funt in the lobby the previous evening, he told her that this was the only excursion scheduled for the morrow.

"I'm sure you will fit in, Ms. Peen," Funt had assured her. "We plan for all ages and abilities. And the beach is magnificent."

Now, in the dim light of dawn—it was only 9:30—Devilly lined up with a group of much younger octos waiting for their transport. She eyed them with envy: muscular males, supple females, and the usual smatter of awkward in-betweeners. She tried to straighten the slightly crinkled frill on the margin of her mantle and heard—or thought she heard—a suppressed giggle from behind her.

The resort's SeaRover arrived, driven by a

buff young octo wearing a torn *Ripples* logo.

"*¡Hola!* Guys, I'm Tydewater Bondy—call me 'Tye'. I am your driver, guide, and instructor for today. Three for the price of one! Super cool to see you all."

"I have got one more for you, Tydewater," interrupted Funt. "This is Ms. Devilly Peen."

"Right on! Hi, 'Dev'. Now hold on!"

The group clutched the taxi tightly in a happy tangle of suckers, while considerately leaving a little circle around Devilly.

In the rush of bubbles, Devilly's chief concern was to maintain her grip as they sped through the shallows. She gathered from listening to the chatter that Silver Sands on the windward side of *Isla Florida* was known for its reliable break. What this might be remained, for Devilly, a mystery.

Rounding a rock, they were buffeted by turbulence from breakers rolling inshore through a gap in the barrier reef.

"Nearly there!" cried Tye. "Looks like surf's up!"

Indeed. They halted in the shelter of an isolated coral head, and the octopods disembarked. Devilly found herself rolling back and forth on the bottom in time with the passing waves.

"Rip currents are going to be strong, so make sure you get in them after you land on the beach. They'll suck you back out here in no time!"

Around Devilly, everyone was collecting a sheet of plastic from the rear of the SeaRover. Everyone seemed to know what to do. Devilly looked around helplessly.

"Here 'Dev', you'll need a plasty," called Tye, seeing Devilly's bewilderment. He handed her a long sliver of plastic sheeting.

"Suckers on." Tye arranged Devilly's tentacles on the board. She clutched tight, looking through the transparent plastic at the sandy bottom.

"Remember to hold your breath, Dev, when you are above the surface. Now I'll lift you up when a good wave comes, then jet as fast as you can."

Against the roar of the surf, Devilly's protests fell on deaf ears. Tye gave her a thumbs up and a strong push. She felt herself lifted by the front of the rising wave. The ripples on the sandy bottom seemed to accelerate backwards. Devilly jetted frantically: she caught the wave and stopped struggling, letting the wave carry her towards the shore.

It was quite a thrill, Devilly decided. Effortless.

The wave broke, Devilly parted with her board, and she was flung into a chaos of churning water, spinning, tumbling in the wash; one moment above the surface, the next dragging along the bottom. She couldn't breathe the froth. Was this the end? It seemed an age before she felt the power of the wave diminish. She bumped along the bottom, rolling over and over until the wave tired and withdrew, leaving her sprawled on the sand. She was in the open air!

"For a first timer, that was really good." Tye slid to a halt beside her. "Next wave, remember to bail before the break."

Ah, thought Devilly, the break. She should have asked.

She glanced up and down the beach. The sand really was silver, and strangely slippery.

She looked more closely.

"Yeah," said Tye, seeing her examine the beach. "Microplastic. It's great: hardly any abrasions when you hit the shore. Kinda cool, those dunes at the back of the beach too—all plastic. But don't try climbing up there. No traction!"

Devilly had no intention of doing so, but was still gazing up at the plastic dunes admiring their sheen, when Tye shouted,

"Whoa! Here comes a biggy!"

Devilly spun about to see a wall of foam rushing towards them. She had no time to brace before it hit, sweeping her further up the beach towards the slippery dunes. God, she will be stranded at the high tide mark!

Almost spent, the wave dragged her sideways and then back down the beach towards the sea.

"Just relax," she heard Tye call. "You're in the rip!"

Struggle was useless, and Devilly let the current carry into the deeper water. She rode up and over the incoming rollers before, once a good distance from shore, she let herself sink back to the bottom. The others were already there, gathered in the shelter of the coral head, chatting excitedly about their rides.

"Super cool! I'm going to go again—did you see that seventh wave? It was ginormous—That beach is sick!"

Devilly watched the youngsters float to the surface and hang, waiting for the next wave. No thank you. She let herself drift alongshore towards the point of rock they had rounded on arrival. There, the waves lost much of their height and energy. In the calm of this bay, the rollers barely crested but flopped exhausted onto the sand.

Devilly made a few tentative attempts to catch another wave. She finally succeeded and rode her plasty all the way to the beach, where she sat in the foam and out of the wind. From here she could watch the flashes of colour as the other surfers showed off in the big waves further down the beach.

The sun went in suddenly, and even in the shallows washed by the warm surf, Devilly felt a chill. A shelf of cloud was spreading across the sky from the west, and out to sea a dark line presaged an approaching squall. She had best rejoin the others.

She found Tye swimming around gathering his charges.

"Listen up, guys. There is a red flag up now. Seems a storm is blowing in."

A groan went up from the group.

"I know it's a bummer, but we need to get back around the headland ASAP. The way the tide sets, we won't make it back before dark if we don't leave now."

Devilly felt a flood of relief. Her entire skin was tingling, and she knew that she would be shaking plastic beads out of her mantle for hours. Still, she could tick surfing off her bucket list.

✦　✦　✦

THE SEAROVER WAS making slow progress against the current as they made their way back towards the resort. After the sunshine of the morning, the dark cloud now cast a shadow over the choppy water, dampening their earlier euphoria. Tye took them close inshore, where a long finger of reef offered some shelter and a counter-current carried them in the right direction. They jetted over a hurrying set of mega-ripples, skimming up one side, down into the hollow and up again like a roller coaster. Devilly began to feel queasy.

Tye suddenly cut the jets and they glided to a halt, bobbing in mid-water above a field of sand ridges and hollows. Peering over the driver's shoulder, Devilly could see a white bundle near the bottom of the hollow directly ahead, tugged back and forth by the oscillating current.

"Is that a body?" whispered the young octo beside Devilly.

They came closer. Now they could make out the stumps of tentacles and the remains of the mantle, pallid in death with all recognizable features nibbled away.

"There's another one!"

Sure enough, when Devilly looked where her neighbour pointed, she saw a second bundle in the next sand hollow.

"There's another, and another!
"Jesus."

"Tye! Get us out of here!"

Their driver needed no encouragement but stalled the engine in his eagerness. The current carried them inexorably over a graveyard; hollow after hollow held its pale burden. Tye finally got the jets to catch. He pushed forward the throttle and they headed back into deeper water.

An hour later, after struggling against the turbulent tide, and with their skins raw from sun and surf, the surfing expedition slumped wearily into the lobby of *Ripples*, exhausted and distressed. They were greeted by Serafin Funt and Pleća Kalamarnica, the latter bedraggled and looking even more angry than usual. Unsurprising, thought Devilly who remembered from reading the Events of the Day that Pleća had charge of "Funsters", an activity advertised to parents who wished rid of their youngsters for a whole afternoon.

"Ah, the surfers return! I trust you all had a 'funt' time, haha." His voice trailed off as he registered their grim demeanor. Tye hurried Funt to one side to report their gruesome discovery.

After a hurried discussion, during which Devilly overheard Funt tell Tye "No, absolutely not!", the Assistant Manager turned to address the group.

"You have all had a dreadful shock. Pleća will find you some blankets and rustle up something hot to drink. I will call the authorities. They will wish to interview you and I ask that you all stay here in the lobby until they arrive."

"Aw," said one of the surfers. "That's not cool man."

"Yeah," shouted another. "How about a refund?"

"I counted thirty corpses rolling on the bottom," added Devilly.

Chapter 10

"THEY ARE SAYING it was migrants." Blenny Musselshuck was leaning towards Devilly over their sachets of tea with all the familiarity of a friend who had shared and survived an excursion by *Ochas Lagunas*. They were sitting in the cafeteria.

"When we were in the Old Quarter, I was saying to Lemi that I wouldn't want to live here. Not always, I mean. Everyone seems so poor . . ."

Devilly heard sirens announcing the police.

"And then there was that awful business last revolution when all those bodies washed up on the Gyre. You remember? Trafficking, they said. Gangs."

"It shouldn't be allowed," she added, settling complacently into her nook.

"I think I should go to the lobby," said Devilly, putting down her sachet and rising to take her leave. "The police will want to interview everybody."

"Well, you must tell me all when you get back," replied Blenny, eagerly. "Lemi says we should try to fly out tomorrow, but I say we tough it out. I would feel terrible if we weren't here to support you."

Devilly scooted rather quickly out of the cafeteria and into the lobby where a pair of uniforms were trying to make some order of the confusion.

"*Señores! Por favor!* Please to line up. We will take name and room number one at a time."

She recognized Sergeant Caracol near the entrance. She sidled around the waving mass of tentacles towards him.

"Ah, Señora Peen,' said the sergeant on seeing Devilly. "How terrible for this to happen on your holiday!"

"Yes, but worse for your tourist trade, I'm afraid. Tell me, Sergeant, is this another accident with migrants."

"*Si*, Señora. It is likely. They build a small raft, maybe with plastic bottles scrounged from the beaches, and think they can sail all the way to the Gyre. It is foolish, *¡estúpido!* There are many dangers. If lose power and plastic cement weakens, raft falls apart. They are left floating in mid-ocean; a storm comes, a shark and *finito*."

"Economic migrants, I suppose."

"*Sí.* But bad criminals too. Lot of money." Caracol looked across the lobby to where a surfer was arguing loudly with his constable.

"Please excuse me, Señora. You need not wait here and are free to go, but please to stay within the resort."

✧ ✧ ✧

BACK IN HER accommodation, Devilly flopped on the floor. Every muscle ached. Perhaps she should just close her eyes and fall asleep as she lay. But she couldn't banish the memory of the pale bodies washing in the surf. It was she who had insisted that Tye drive slowly around the sand plain to see the extent of the calamity, and also—in the off chance—of finding a survivor. No one else seemed to have a clue what to do and deferred to her obvious age and authority. She secured the latter by descending from the SeaRover and examining one of the corpses closely. It was in an early stage of decay, and only a handful of crustaceans had arrived—how they sense the arrival of dinner, the Lord knows.

Returning to the group, she had brushed away one of the undertaker shrimp that had hopefully attached itself to her mantle.

"Dead a day at least, and no sign of violence. I'm guessing they drowned far out to sea, judging from the bite marks." Devilly had thoroughly researched drowning for a Daisy Cuttle mystery and had spent several profitable hours examining cases with her pathologist friend, one of the weekenders who came down to Nether Vortex to escape the big city.

"Yes, if they had drowned near the shore, the crabs would have got to them sooner."

She saw the look of horror on the faces of the young surfers. After her day wrestling awkwardly with her plasty among carefree youth carving impossible tricks on the waves, she congratulated herself. Respect, finally. Respect.

Chapter 11

NEXT MORNING, SNUGGLED in her nest of bubblewrap and sucking a sachet of breakfast tea, Devilly planned a leisurely day. She would call room service for breakfast and later fancied a massage at the Spa. The previous two days had been eventful, and she had no intention of committing to any more organized activities.

The telephone beside her bed rang. The instrument emitted streams of bubbles—pulses of burbling sound, shrill and impossible to ignore. Resentful at being disturbed, she reached over and suckered the receiver to her ear.

"Yes."

"This is the Front Desk, Señora Peen. There are two officers here who would like to speak to you."

Damn. Of course, there would be more

questions about yesterday.

"I'll come to the lobby directly."

Devilly got up and went to check her appearance in the polished nacre of the bathroom—a suggestion of wrinkles around the eyes, and some sag in the mantle that she hoped others would not notice. The lighting in these bathrooms was really too bright. She flexed her tentacles and suitably muted her colouration for an encounter with Authority.

Minutes later, Devilly glided into the lobby. She didn't recognize the two waiting policemen. Doubtless after the discovery of the previous evening, her friendly sergeant would be tied up with paperwork.

"Señora Peen?"

"Yes, I mean "*Sí*". This is about yesterday, I suppose. How can I help you, officers?"

"The Señora is to accompany us to police headquarters," replied one of the policemen while the other stared at her blankly. "Come, we have vehicle outside."

"Well, I . . . Yes, of course." Devilly looked around. The lobby was empty of other tourists, and the desk clerk avoided her eye. "Perhaps I should leave a message . . ."

"*Vamos!* The *Jefe* is not a patient man."

       ❖   ❖   ❖

OUTSIDE THE RESORT lobby, a nagging current tugged at Devilly as the officers escorted her. A choppy sea allowed mere glints of early morning light to penetrate the water. She felt cold—the storm had stirred up water from the depths beyond the barrier reef. It was not a morning to be dragged out of bed by the police. Oh, don't exaggerate, Devilly reminded herself. It is probably routine, and one cannot expect courtesy from all ranks.

They jetted inshore across the shallow lagoon, passing swiftly over sand mottled with patches of sea grass. Police headquarters was set back from the main tourist development with its gated resorts. Here in the *barrio* Devilly glimpsed the seedy side of *Isla Florida*. Shoddy looking tenements crowded along the borders of the channel they sped through— flimsy constructions of corrugated plastic glued to the hard ground by encrusting growths.

The police driver curved to the right, and Devilly looked obliquely down at a pattern of rectangles on the seabed. Their edges stood out like knives in the crisp morning light, despite the efforts of encrusting marine growth to smooth their geometry. Devilly had read of researchers finding the foundations of Arboreal buildings around the island. Perhaps she was seeing the remains of walls?

A jetsam of plastic and other refuse stirred in the current. She could see children playing. Here was poverty such as she had glimpsed in Tire Town, although most who dwelled here, Devilly supposed, would have service jobs in the tourist industry.

She sensed they were arriving. They sank slowly to the sea floor within one of the larger rectangles. From above, the walls had seemed solid, but now appeared riddled with cavities, their black interiors in harsh contrast with the surrounding white calcrete.

"This way, Señora."

The officers led Devilly towards one of the larger entrances. The senior of her two escorts waved a tentacle at the guard, and they penetrated the midden. Devilly soon lost all sense of direction as their route twisted through tunnels of dead coral. The tunnel walls of a hard and rough, surfaces foreign to the world of smooth plastic she was familiar with on the Gyre.

"Please to wait in here, Señora."

Devilly squeezed into a small oblong interview room, bare except for three plastic stools around a plain table. A small red light blinked in the corner of an opaque screen at one end. Otherwise, there was nothing to relieve the eye; all encrusting marine life had been scrubbed from the walls. Her escort slammed shut the clam shell that served as a door, and departed, leaving Devilly alone to think and to worry.

What would Daisy Cuttle do in such circumstances? Devilly's fictional private detective would rise to the occasion, she decided, and formulate a Plan. Daisy would open the clam with a shucker hidden in her mantle, and make her way unerringly back to the outside, where she would escape pursuit by emitting a thick cloud of ink. She would fall in with a band of plucky resistance fighters plotting to overthrow a dictator, or perhaps meet a rugged police inspector determined to fight corruption, or foil criminal gangs that had taken over the reef. But she wasn't under arrest, was she? Perhaps all this fuss was just normal procedure.

"Ah, *Buenos dias*, Señora Peen."

Someone thrust aside the clam shell, and she turned to see Comandante Pesquero in the doorway.

"Comandante, I am very happy to see you. There seems to have been some misunderstanding..."

"Do not be alarmed, Señora." The Comandante settled on the stool across the table from Devilly and placed a slim dossier in front of him. A corporal stayed floating to attention behind him.

"We merely have a few more questions about yesterday."

"Well, of course, but was it really necessary..."

"Are you acquainted with a Señor Alexander McKelpie?" Pesquero took a photograph from a file and pushed it across the table.

"No, I mean Yes. Sandy, you mean?"

"When did you last see Señor McKelpie?"

"I, er, the day before yesterday. I saw him in the lobby bar."

"The barkeep suggests you were having an intimate conversation with him."

Devilly flushed pink.

"What? No, that is ridiculous. He insisted on buying me a drink, but then I left."

"You didn't see him again that evening."

"Certainly not!"

"Is there anyone else that can verify that?"

This was outrageous.

"Now, Comandante, all I did was have a drink; I left; I went to bed. Alone. Next morning, I got up and joined the expedition to Silver Sands where we found thirty bodies in the surf. I'm just about fed up with your innuendos. What is this all about?"

"Thirty-one," replied the Comandante.

"I'm sorry?"

"Thirty-one bodies. Thirty *emigrados*, drowned when their pathetic raft came unstuck in mid-ocean—and one Dr. Alexander McKelpie.

And I was one of the last to see him, thought Devilly. The police officers were watching her intensely. She knew they expected a reaction: shock at the loss of a good friend, or guilty fear. She knew she should express emotion, but her expression remained blank.

"How did you identify the corpse?" Devilly knew from her research that drowning victims soon lost all colouration, leaving a pallid mass of flesh that made recognition difficult, even for close relatives.

"Señora, you do not seem surprised by this news. We identified your friend by the brown bracelet around the stub of one of his remaining tentacles."

Yes, of course. She had seen Sandy put on the bracelet when they had registered together. He must have been in the water for less than twenty-four hours.

"How was he killed?"

"Señora Peen, perhaps you have forgotten who is asking the questions? Now I must ask you to turn out the contents of your mantle."

This was awkward. Devilly, as she rummaged in the recesses of her mantle, regretting the reference collection of samples that she always carried in her poison sac. She lined them up on the table.

"This isn't what it looks like," she assured the Comandante. "I always carry these with me. They are essential to my writing. I need them for research . . ."

"This label reads 'deadly cone shell venom'."

"Yes, and I have the antidote right here. Accidents on the reef can be fatal. This could save a life!"

"I see."

There was silence as they both regarded the array of small vials and sachets.

"Very well, Señora. I must leave you now for a little while. This officer will stay here. He will bring tea."

The Comandante gathered his papers, bunched his tentacles, and left the interview room.

✧   ✧   ✧

AN HOUR PASSED, then two. Devilly was angry with herself. She should have demanded to contact the consulate; she must insist on a lawyer. Or call the Resort and speak to the Manager; even send a message to the Gyre and ask her nephew for help. He was police too and would have influence with the authorities. But she might only be allowed one phone call. Which then? This holiday was becoming a nightmare! The tea they had provided was vile.

Finally, after what seemed to her an age, Devilly heard a commotion outside the door. The clam swung open, and the Comandante entered, followed by an octo in plain clothes.

"Señora, a thousand apologies for keeping you waiting. This is proving a most difficult case."

Devilly felt the relief flooding over her, her skin cooling.

"I accept your apology, Comandante. Thirty-one bodies overnight would tax the resources of any organization."

Comandante Pesquero coughed, a little embarrassed.

"This gentleman is Major Siphon."

Devilly looked at the newcomer. Surely, she had seen him before? Yes—he was the hunched figure she remembered, the one with lousy camouflage.

"You were in the Sea Fan, at the bar!"

"Indeed, and I can testify that the evening was as you have described to the Comandante. But I get ahead of myself. You may remember my name; I was involved in the Clamshucker affair last year that you helped resolve."

"Oh yes, now I come to think of it, my nephew Inspector Moray mentioned that someone high up in Centro had tried to influence the enquiry."

"Hm. Not exactly. But yes, I am that Major Siphon, but please, it is 'Lionel'. I resigned from the Service shortly afterwards to go into the private sector. I am here in that new capacity. My job is to investigate insurance fraud for MerryVac Assurance."

"I hope you didn't resign because of me."

"Good Grief, no. It was the salary and bonuses."

"Perhaps, if you permit me," interrupted Comandante Pesquero, "my office is much more comfortable than this interview room. If you would follow me . . ."

✧   ✧   ✧

THE OFFICE OF the *Jefe* looked out across the plaza where a group of disconsolate squid sporting bright orange were sweeping the rectangle of coral sand free of debris. Convicts or community service? Devilly wondered. On the far side of the square crowded the plastic roofs of shanties erected in the lee of one of curious walls that she had noticed before.

Pesquero was suggesting wine to go with the crab snacks that an apologetic Sergeant Caracol had laid on the table before them.

"This," he said, holding up a green bottle, "I had imported from the Gyre. It is a wine that rested for many years at the bottom of the sea and recovered from the Shallows by dredging. It was lost, one must suppose, in shipwreck. I have been keeping it for a special occasion."

Pesquero wrestled with a syringe to extract wine from the bottle and insert the blood red fluid into a pair of finely wrought plastic sachets for his guests to suck from.

"Major Siphon has convinced me that we need your experience of poisons, Señora, to explain Señor McKelpie's death. You are, of course, free to go, but I would take is as a personal favour if you would lend your expertise to the investigation."

"Of course, Commandante. If I could have my collection back?"

"Caracol!" shouted Pesquero through the door. "See that the Signora's possessions are returned immediately."

"Now, to business." He turned and lifted his sachet. "*Salud!* To the celebrated author Señora Peen."

"And to her creation Daisy Cuttle," added Siphon. "An inspiration to us all."

Chapter 12

A POLICE DRIVER had taken Devilly and Major Siphon back to Ripples, the apologies of his superior still ringing in their ears.

"Let me buy you lunch," said Lionel when they were standing in the lobby.

"It's an all-inclusive," replied Devilly, "so there is really no need. But I would like something to eat. I missed breakfast."

As they were hesitating in the middle of the floor, the Assistant Manager came over to them.

"I am sorry you have had such a distressing experience, Ms. Peen," said Serafin Funt. "Is there anything, anything the resort can do so you can enjoy the rest of your stay with us in peace?"

"No, really. Well, perhaps the spa and massage?"

"Of course. And you, Sir, I don't believe you

are staying at the resort. Perhaps I may give you this visitor's bracelet? It is good for the day as a guest of Ms. Peen."

Devilly and her companion watched Funt retreat behind the reception counter.

"I think we should try to find somewhere quieter to eat," suggested Siphon.

"Yes, the cafeteria is not really the place to discuss murder. I would like to try a restaurant away from the resort. It seems to be the same menu here every day."

"There is a very good sushi place just up the road."

"Is it expensive?"

"Not a problem. One of the benefits of not working for the government. I have an expense account. No, I insist . . ."

A five-minute taxi ride and they arrived. The restaurant was obviously expensive, one of those where the food circulated in tiny boats. This was a novel experience for Devilly, who seldom ate out, and then at the pub in Nether Vortex. After some failed attempts, she mastered the technique of lassoing morsels from the moving stream. Siphon ordered saki.

"So, why were you at the Sea Fan the other night?" asked Devilly. "What exactly are you investigating that brings you here?"

"Hm," said Siphon, turning away from her, and gazing at an angel fish pecking at one of the restaurant's ornamental anemones. "Yes, I see I must give you some context. It all relates to a larger investigation. As you may know, MerryVac is the largest insurer for travel, life and medical on the Gyre. Our database is large, so the excess deaths we have measured are statistically significant. More people are dying at resorts by *Ochas Lagunas* than should be."

"You mean you are paying out too much?"

"Indeed. It has accumulated over the years to quite a large amount."

Devilly vaguely remembered that her own life policy paid half a million clams if she met with a fatal accident. These excess deaths must have cost the company millions. Or perhaps not: her premiums had risen steadily over the years. She had put that down to her advancing years.

After a desert of some algal confection, followed by diluted espressos, Devilly was feeling quite replete. Lionel called for the bill, and she glimpsed the outrageous total. At least Siphon was paying, presumably at MerryVac's expense.

"Let me jet back with you," said Lionel. "It really isn't far, and the coral borders along the boulevard are quite fine."

When they arrived at *Ripples*, they did not go into the lobby but drifted in the garden, still discussing the case.

"My prime suspect is dead," admitted Lionel Siphon, a touch bitterly. "I was ninety percent sure I had my man. He had opportunity, visiting every resort owned by *Ochas Lagunas* over the last several years. But I admit there was no consistent means—all the deceased seem to have died under completely different circumstances—and as to motif, I had no idea. If McKelpie was not the perpetrator, then why is he a victim? I am back to square one."

"You seem sure that these deaths are not accidental?"

"Yes, but contrived to look like accidents. A resort can always expect one or two of the older guests to expire during their stays, especially if they are encouraged to undertake inappropriate activities."

Devilly winced at the implied criticism.

"But the Comandante believes that Sandy's death must be linked to that criminal gang, *Los Picos* or whatever they call themselves—those responsible for people smuggling."

Siphon gave a long bubbling snort.

"He would think that. He is a provincial policeman and inevitably sees matters through the lens of local crime. I believe the murderer took advantage of the carnage to dispose of the body, hoping that it would be overlooked. What is one more among so many?"

"Did they determine cause of death?"

"They do have pathologists here on the island, but I'm afraid that they are out of their depth. For McKelpie, the verdict was drowning, along with the others."

"You are not convinced?"

"That is why I persuaded Pesquero that you should look at the body."

"What on earth for?"

"I told him that the study of marine poisons is your specialty, and that at Gyre Centro, they highly respect Devilly Peen's opinion. Pesquero came around quite quickly. He is something of a fan of yours; it seems he admires your *Sting of Medusa*."

"Well, yes," replied Devilly. "In that case, Daisy Cuttle narrowed down the suspects by . . ."

"I never read fiction," said Siphon.

Devilly was a little taken aback. One comes across such people.

"I suppose you can be thankful that the thirty *emigrados* didn't take out policies with MerryVac," she said tartly.

Chapter 13

T HE ASSISTANT MANAGER was embarrassed.

"I am sorry Ms. Peen, but I have a communication for you at Reception. I am afraid that in yesterday's confusion, the staff omitted to give it to you."

Devilly followed the Assistant Manager to the front desk, feeling a little self-conscious. She had dressed for the morgue, in a somber pattern of green and brown. However, Funt made no comment, and none in the colourful group in the lobby seemed to notice.

"Here we are, Ms. Peen," said Funt, reaching to extract an envelope from behind the counter.

"Thank you," said Devilly. Glancing down, she saw it was by hand delivery with the *Ripples* logo. It would keep—a bill for extras, in all likelihood.

"Perhaps you would call me a taxi?"

Minutes later, Devilly was cruising along the edge of the barrier, the now familiar boulevard with its repetition of hotel, resort, condo apartment. Continuing on this route would, she knew, lead to the jetport but the driver swerved in-shore towards the hospital. Peering over his shoulder, Devilly could see a dead patch reef ahead. *El hospital general* was in water so shallow that the corals had been abandoned by their symbiotic algae leaving it stark and white.

Devilly had arranged to meet Major Siphon before the main entrance.

"Stop!" she called. "*¡Aqui, aqui!*"

"You are just on time," said Siphon, as Devilly fumbled to find clams for the fare. "The Comandante is waiting for us inside."

Together, they jetted through the lobby. Here the water was murky and faintly yellowish, an unpleasant change from the blue lagoon outside. No current penetrated here: it was hot, and the water tasted of disinfectant. A line of patients propped themselves against one wall— Devilly knew from her experience in the Gyre, that those cases missing less than four tentacles were technically ambulatory. Here the rule seemed more relaxed—one unfortunate seemed entirely wrapped in new skin, anxious eyes peering through thin slits in the covering. Day surgery, she guessed.

"Down here," said Siphon, leading the way. They entered a slanting tunnel that got ever stuffier as they descended. At the base of the slope, he pushed aside a curtain of weed.

"Here we are, Comandante."

Pesquero had been conversing with a green-garbed medico and looked up at their entrance. He ignored Siphon and addressed Devilly directly.

"*Buenos dias*, Señora Peen. This is all most regrettable, and not, I imagine, what you expected of your holiday on *Isla Florida*. But your reputation goes before you. Major Siphon convinces me that you can help determine the cause of death of the unfortunate Alexander McKelpie."

The Comandante signaled to an assistant, who gingerly pulled the cover from the nearest corpse.

Devilly had been bracing herself but was

still shocked to see the condition of the body. What was once corpulent and robust had been reduced to a flaccid bag of fluid. In this state of decomposition, the corpse had to be tethered to the gurney to prevent it from floating away. Chromatophores that, when McKelpie was alive, had flashed the clashing colours of the McKelpie tartan had lost their potency and reverted to a ghostly grey. One of the eyes had been nibbled by crustacea, while the other gazed unfocused through Devilly, she who only two days ago had been the subject of its eager interest. She thrust aside the thought.

"I'll need to explore with my tentacle."

Through strict discipline and trial and error, Devilly had honed a tentacle tip into a sensitive diagnostic tool. With it, she could taste a poison for comparison with the reference collection tucked in her poison sac. She had doubts that she would be successful—there must be substances here on the reef that she had never encountered.

Siphon and Pesquero drifted away from the corpse to give Devilly room. She inserted her thinnest tentacle into the slash left by the hospital pathologist and wriggled it back and forth to sample as much of McKelpie's body fluid as possible.

"Señora, this is really too much to ask…" began the Comandante. "*Madre mia!*" He turned away abruptly. Devilly on penetrating the siphon, had dislodged a sea louse that scampered away frantically.

Devilly withdrew from the body. She had certainly tasted something. Now it would be up to one of her subsidiary brains—the one tasked with archiving—to find a similar expression in her reference collection.

"We might as well swim up to fresher waters," said Devilly. Her companions hastily agreed.

"It is clearly a class of marine venom," said Devilly, five minutes later. "But it does not match anything in my experience."

"There is still a trace of poison in the body—well-rinsed, obviously, and the concentration has diminished with time. I suggest that when first administered, it would have been enough to render the victim unconscious. The drowning came later, through siphonic constriction."

"So, Señora, a drowning after poisoning. Our pathologist was partially correct." The Comandante was still hoping to pin it on *Los Picos*.

"If you wish, Comandante, I could test the other thirty."

"No, no, Señora. That will not be necessary!"

"What is it likely to be?" asked Siphon. "One of those venomous fish?"

"You mean like the Golden Lion? Possibly."

"Is that the one with the spines?" asked the Comandante.

"The autopsy noted puncture marks," mused Devilly. "But after rolling over sea urchins, corals and so on, the skin was pretty torn up. So that is hardly surprising."

"But Señora, surely this could have been accidental? Your poor friend must have been stabbed by this fish," objected the Comandante, "and then succumbed."

Siphon interrupted with a characteristic snort.

"I think, Comandante, that it might be better to consider this a deliberate act as Ms. Peen suggests, rather than an accident. It would not help for the Press to learn that these dangerous fish are loose on your reef."

"If it is a fish," replied Devilly, dubiously. "But I believe I can narrow down the poison with a little research. If I do, it may help you find the supplier."

Poor Sandy McKelpie, thought Devilly, as she rode back to *Ripples*. He was such a fan and would have been delighted to be the principal in a murder mystery.

Chapter 14

ELIMINATE THE METAMORPH is the first rule of detecting, according to the Daisy Cuttle formula. Otherwise, one could blame everything on the shape-shifter; any murder on the butler. It does not make for a thrilling plot.

Metamorphs, that symbiont species who had traveled to earth with the octopods, are hard to live with, but impossible to do without. Their origin lay in genetic meddling back in the Middle Ages. Some claimed they were half octopod; no one ventured what the other half might be, not in polite society anyway.

Devilly prided herself on her nose for metamorphs. One could always tell, she maintained; the shifting façade and the transparency of expression gave them away. Henri, her previous, was a case in point; Lawrence, her current, gave himself away by his sheer inconstancy. But here at *Ripples*, she had not sensed the presence of any metamorphs. All she encountered seemed on the spectrum from 100 percent octopod to full cuttle. If Lem Musselshuck was a metamorph, for instance, she would vent all her ink.

Which left a big problem for Devilly. Absent a metamorph to blame, who had both motif and opportunity to kill? Despite the intriguing appeal of Major Siphon's theory of an international insurance scam, she was beginning to think that the Comandante might be right in thinking that McKelpie had run afoul of *Los Picos*. Her conversation with Monsieur Le Pieuff had left her with the strong impression that organized crime was rampant on *Isla Florida*.

Which reminded Devilly: she had promised the Comandante to investigate further the poison in the good doctor's remains. The toxin was not like any she had in her collection, but there was something familiar about it. What she needed was something to jog her memory. The catalogue given to her by Monsieur Le Pieuff lay on the coffee table. She picked it up and scanned the list: cone venom; dried garlands of men-of-war; extracts from assorted nudi-branchs. Now, here was a promising entry: the Death Frill, she read, was a sea slug, pure white with green spots, its poison lethal if injected in minute quantities. Rare and only found on certain remote reefs around *Isla Florida*, it was not recommended for amateur collectors. Supplies were limited.

Devilly took a sip of clamtini from the mini-bar and put the catalogue aside. The Death Frill could be the culprit! She would inform the police that Monsieur Le Pieuff's emporium might be a useful lead. Sweeping some stray Perrier bottles beneath her, she settled more comfortably; *Ripples*, at least, did not skimp on the quality of plastic. But something nagged her. Sometimes memory was a diffuse matter for an octopod, swirling around and around.

It was the brain at the base of her third ten-tacle that reminded Devilly. The envelope! She fumbled through her mantle pouches until she retrieved it. Although somewhat pulped, the addressee was still legible:

To Ms. Devilly Peen, Private and Confidential.

The note inside was written in purple ink: it struck Devilly as a curiously childish script—all loops and carefully rounded letters.

Dear Ms. Peen, since parting in the bar last evening, I am reminded that you expressed a desire to explore the front of the barrier reef. I have taken the liberty of booking two places on the upcoming adventure tour offered by the resort. It is, I am given to understand, not to be missed. The River of Jewels is, so they claim, holds the finest specimens of coral on the reef. I look forward to the privilege of escorting you. Yours affectionately,

A. (Sandy) McKelpie.

Affectionately! Well, he certainly had a warm personality, poor fellow. Frankly, another adventure like Silver Sands she could do without. No, a morning doing nothing would suit just fine.

But it was not to be: the phone rang.

"*Buenos dias*, Señora. I have the Comandante Pesquero on the line."

"Hello?"

"Señora Peen? I trust you have recovered from your adventures. Have you by any chance had the time to analyze further the substance you detected?"

"Yes, Comandante, I was about to ring you. I believe the toxin used to dispatch Dr. McKelpie might have been sold at a place in the Old Quarter. A shop run by a Monsieur Le Pieuff."

"Ah indeed? We know Monsieur Le Pieuff. A slippery customer. French."

"He seemed to be having issues with *Los Picos* when I was there."

"Good, *bueno*. But let me reassure you. We did a sweep of Tire Town and the *barrio* last night. I have several *Los Picos* in our cells. It is only a matter of time before they confess to the murder of Señor McKelpie.

"But Comandante, why would *Los Picos* want to kill him?"

"Alas, it is common here. A matter of wrong place, wrong time. Now Señora, there is another favour I must ask you."

"Yes, of course, Comandante."

"We have tried without success to discover

relatives of Señor McKelpie."

"He never mentioned any family to me. He seems to have spent his retirement traveling alone to various resorts."

"*Si, si*, that is also our conclusion. So, to my request. In this warm tropical water of ours, molluscan bodies dissolve rapidly, especially in that hospital morgue with its ineffectual climate control. Soon only the beak remains."

"Well, that is also true on the Gyre. Even in temperate waters . . ."

"*Exactemente.* It is usual for the family to make the arrangements, but Señora, it seems that you are the only one here on *Isla Florida* who knew Señor McKelpie."

"I, er . . . I would not say I knew him. He was a casual acquaintance."

"*Excelente!* As an acquaintance, I would be most obligated if you would take charge of the remains. I can assure you that the package is small and light. Sergeant Caracol will bring it to *Ripples* directly. Again, Señora Peen, your assistance has been invaluable. I am confident we will soon have a confession, and your friend will be revenged."

"He was not really a friend . . ."

Pesquero rang off. Devilly put back the receiver on its cradle. Damn it: what a bore! As a rule, she was wary of striking up casual acquaintances. Now, just being polite on the flight had come back to haunt her with a vengeance. She held with one tentacle the invitation to go snorkeling on the reef from an overbearing Lothario twice her age, and soon in another she would be carrying his mortal remains for disposal God knows where.

Devilly's second clamtini proved fruitful: after mulling possibilities, she stumbled on an obvious solution! Back on the Gyre, a funeral consisted of bidding farewell to the departed by releasing the beak to fall gently down through the water into the abyss, where it would lie for millennia in the bottom ooze. It was a peaceful rite, usually followed by crab sandwiches and libations. Here in the lagoon, that would be inappropriate and probably against municipal regulations, but perhaps at the edge of the barrier reef where the bottom dropped off rapidly? If she flung it out as far as possible? Devilly sighed: she would have to accept McKelpie's invitation, after all.

Chapter 15

SERAFIN FUNT HAD just finished writing out the day's activities on a chalkboard in the lobby. As he wiped his hands fastidiously, he admired his handiwork—each letter firmly fashioned. Even those guests poor of sight could read that the reef exploration experience would leave at eleven. Funt's handwriting should be good, he thought bitterly; his father had supervised his early efforts with the lash of the tentacle.

The reef experience was well subscribed, he saw with satisfaction. He had twelve on his list and had had no trouble filling the place reserved for McKelpie. He wondered whether the doctor's "plus 1" would turn up.

But here was Ms. Peen, as he hoped.

"Ah, Ms. Peen. Back for more punishment? I can assure you that our reef tour is much less strenuous than surfing." He smiled widely, and finned backwards so that Devilly could read the notice.

"Yes, Signor Funt. I have a reservation, purchased by the late Dr. McKelpie, I believe."

"Yes, the good doctor made the arrangement. May he rest in peace." Funt gave a slight deferential bow. "But I was not sure Madam would attend."

"The doctor is not resting in peace yet, Funt. That is why I am here. I wanted to ask you if there would be any difficulty in releasing his remains out beyond the barrier."

What delicious irony, thought Funt.

"Of course. Of course. That is quite possible. I can arrange for a quiet moment away from the group for you to say your goodbyes."

"Good, so at eleven here in the lobby?"

"Indeed. Indeed. And today I will have the pleasure of accompanying you. The trip will be led by Tye Bondy—who you know from surfing. Tye is our dive master. Pleća will also be coming, so you will be among familiar faces. They are there to help."

He had not planned on attending a funeral for McKelpie—murderers of the deceased were not usually invited on such occasions—but this fell in well with his plans. Dumping the body with the drowning victims—*Los Picos* had been most obliging—should have been a perfect solution, but chance had intervened. Why had he forgotten to detach McKelpie's armband? The old fool should have kept his beak shut about recognizing him from his last position with *Ochas Lagunas*. That had been at the Crumblies Resort when he had disposed of an offensive financier. He smiled at the memory. It had been highly profitable when the insurance eventually paid out, not to mention the pleasure he had derived from planning the "accident". Now, the Peen woman was offering to dispose of what remained of the doctor for him! Life was good!

McKelpie had been a complication, but Funt was not to be deterred from the original plan. Unlike the doctor, Devilly Peen had been thoroughly researched; the existence of her MerryVac policy confirmed, her vulnerabilities identified. She was an elderly pensioner from the shires who had been delighted by the offer of a free vacation. That she wrote murder mysteries added piquancy: Funt had no doubts about his superior intelligence; she would be the victim in the last of her ridiculous romances. He would be doing the reading public a favour! Lure her to the resort of his choice, and then—whack!

However, this would be the last time he ran the insurance scam; that investigator from MerryVac was nosing around. Funt had no idea whether McKelpie had a policy, but now the police had identified the victim, there would be two unexpected deaths at Ripples this season. That might be a problem. Next year he must try something different, and he wondered if kidnap for ransom could be the way to go. There would be much planning to do over the winter.

Meanwhile, his contract ran for another month—another four weeks of catering to the likes of the Musselshucks and Crabbles, not to mention their vile larvae. Come to Captain Fun, you ignorant little creepies. He was always smiling because he was always imagining their disgusting fates. Pity prudence demanded restraint during the season. But that was his discipline. And Serafin Funt knew discipline—he had the stripes from his youth to remind him—and, although having Ms. Peen perish under the raspers of predatory whelks appealed to him, he understood the need for plausible tragedy. The excursion this afternoon would be his opportunity. God, how he reveled in being a psychopath, his brilliant mind lacking the shackle of scruples, and physically fit too.

Chapter 16

SOMETHING WAS NAGGING Devilly as she prepared for the reef experience. She was still stiff from surfing and was in for a long swim today. Despite Funt's assurance that it would be "easy", Devilly thought it wise to empty the deep pockets of her mantle of unnecessary weight. It was only when she felt a crumpled ball in the depths that she remembered the note Sandy McKelpie had written on the flight. She had stuffed it back in her pouch after getting the prescription filled at Monsieur Le Pieuff's and completely forgotten about it.

Now she carefully spread out the message. It was illegible, but that was the point! This was Sandy's handwriting, and the invitation that he had supposedly sent her was in a completely different hand. One was a hurried scrawl; the other a controlled calligraphy, ohs and loops completed with strict attention.

She dialed Reception.

"This is Ms. Peen. Please connect me to Police Headquarters. It is urgent."

Half a minute later, after some laboured explanation, she reached the office of Pesquero. It was a poor line, transmission affected by the clicking of cutlass shrimps in the lagoon.

"*Perdón, señora.* The Comandante is unavailable."

"Well, may I leave a message for him?"

"Is back after 3 pm."

"Yes, but may I leave a message?"

"Message yes. I will tell him."

"Good. It is to tell him I think I now know who..." The line went dead. The shrimp seemed to have won the battle.

No, she thought, anyone could write carefully on a chalk board if they expect a public notice to be easily read. Anyone. But, she worried, could Serafin Funt be the author? Why would Funt impersonate McKelpie? Could Funt be McKelpie's killer? Was Sandy one of the marks in this insurance scam that Lionel Siphon had described?

No, she was getting way ahead of herself.

This sounded too far-fetched, like something out of one of her own novels. Perhaps it was a good thing she hadn't reached the Comandante. He would have ridiculed her suspicions.

Devilly sighed: she must focus on practicalities. One did not need to bring food, but plenty of Sunslime was essential—they expected to spend time on the exposed reef at low tide. Remembering her previous experiences above water, Devilly would take no chances and lather it on thick.

Before leaving for the lobby, she remembered to check the contents of her poison sac. Besides her reference collection of venom samples—all in minute quantities—she carried an assortment of soothing balms. Should someone scratch themselves on a coral or be impaled by an urchin spine, Devilly would have a remedy. She felt a bit maiden-auntish about doing this, but it was better to be prepared than not. Anyway, that was exactly what she was.

✧ ✧ ✧

"BRAVO MS. PEEN!" "Great Morning for it!"

"Hey whatsup?" Those gathering in the lobby had seen Devilly entering and gave her a warm welcome. The group mostly comprised those who had been surfing earlier in the week. They were respectful, as one is of someone comfortable around corpses.

"Great you decided to come with us again, Dev," said Tye, the trip leader. "You just let me know if we are swimming too fast for you," he added in a quieter voice. "We try to keep the group together, but you know . . ."

Pleća Kalamarnica came over.

"Hiya. We have parcel for you at Reception. Police deliver this morning. Please to come with me."

She led Devilly to the front desk, reached over and snagged an urn-shaped package with her tentacle.

"Is Señor McKelpie, no?"

"Shush, Pleća." Devilly took the package and slipped it under her mantle. "No one is supposed to know. Señor Funt didn't want to spoil the mood. He asked me to be discreet, and that he would find the right moment at the edge of the reef when I could slip away and deposit poor Sandy's remains."

"Señor Funt is coming with us?"

"Yes, he told me so yesterday. Wouldn't want to miss the reef experience, he said."

"Is strange. Usually is just Tye and me. Tye won't be pleased. He likes to do his own thing on the reef trip. Now he has supervisor."

"Funt said he was just coming along to watch."

Pleća fiddle-finned in front of Devilly. Something seemed to be worrying her.

"Assistant Manager not so nice, Ms. Peen," she added, in a whisper. "You must be careful."

"How do you mean?"

"I just say, he is not good man."

"But . . . "

The peep of a whistle interrupted them. Tye was assembling the group.

"Hey snorklers, how are we today?"

This was greeted by groans.

"Great. Now I will just give a run-down of our swim today, and then Pleća and I will go through the safety check. Is everyone here?"

"Okay," said Tye, after hearing a murmur of assent. "The timing is right this morning, so we can take the ebbing tide down the channel to the main reef. There we will climb onto the reef top where we will be just above the water. That will be our opportunity to hunt among the pools for rock crabs. If the waves cooperate, we may see the Devil's Blow Pipe in action!"

None of the younger octos seemed inclined to ask, so Devilly interrupted.

"Is that a kind of fish?"

"Great question. No, it's not. The Blow Pipe is an unusual phenom we have right here in front of Ripples. When the sea is up, water rushes into one of the caverns in the outer reef, and explodes upwards into the air, a geyser sometimes twenty or thirty tentacles high. It only happens with the largest waves, but I have been watching the forecast and expect some big swells to be coming in this afternoon."

"And after that," continued Tye, "we go to a ledge I know overlooking the front wall of the reef, then dive down the face. It's kinda deep down there. Now, have any of you gone deep before?"

Two of the surfers held up tentacles. Like Devilly, most lived on the Gyre, where there was little point in diving into the shadowed mid-ocean depths below the floating plastic. Devilly had done it once as a teenage dare and had followed a dangled line down and down into the dimness. At the bottom of the line, she had hung suspended in a deep purple void, imagining a nameless menace swimming just beyond her straining vision. Perhaps she would sit this one out.

"Okay, the thing to remember is that as we descend, colours shift towards purple and mauve until finally all is black. You must remember to change your camo as we go down. Then, after the dive, Pleća here is going to put out some chum. That should attract sharks. Feeding time is quite a spectacle."

"Hey man, a selfie with sharks!"

"Isn't that dangerous?" asked someone.

"No, not if we watch from the safety of the reef, Dev. Later, the returning tide will bring us back into the lagoon, and après-dive drinks in the Sea Fan Bar. Any more questions?"

Pleća whispered something in Tye's ear.

"Oh, yes. One last thing: the Buddy System. When we are out on the reef, and especially for the deep dive, you should all buddy up. Find someone you like and stick with them."

The group paired off rapidly, leaving Devilly hovering alone in mid-lobby, feeling old and stupid.

"I'll be your Buddy, Ms. Peen." Serafin Funt had sidled up beside her. "Shall we?"

Chapter 17

THE CURRENT CARRIED them gently seawards down the avenue of fan corals towards the barrier reef. The sweepings of the lagoon floated alongside—detached weed, plastic bags, and assorted other flotsam being flushed to the open sea. Soon, however, Tye signed that they should clamber onto the bank of coral that marked the inner margin of the main reef. Devilly followed the example of the others and lassoed a stag horn. Sucker by sucker, she hauled herself up.

It was almost slack water by now, and the sea sloshed lazily over the exposed reef. The overlapping plate corals offered little shelter from the brutal midday sun, and Devilly quickly added another layer of Sunslime. The group spread out, sidling from pool to pool, and following Tye in the general direction of the reef front. Only the distant growl of breakers on the outer reef suggested the proximity of the open ocean.

Every so often came a cry of discovery.

"Hey man, check out this clam!"

"Cool fish in this pool, Tye!"

"Crab! Catch it! There she goes!"

They are as excited as children, thought Devilly. Well, most of them were children. She slipped across a ridge of sharp coral into another hollow. A flash of orange and white caught her eye. She lunged but missed, and the fish found refuge in the arms of a giant anemone. She popped her head above water.

"Hey Tye!" she called across to their guide. "Over here!"

Serafin Funt slipped into the same pool as Devilly, examining a plasticized guide to reef fish.

"The scientific name is *Amphiprion*, but I believe the locals call it *el bufón.*"

Startled, Devilly shot backwards, colliding with the far side of the pool.

"Ouch!"

"My dear lady, have you hurt yourself?"

Devilly looked at the back of her number

five tentacle to see a black spine protruding from her skin.

"The spear of a sea egg, I see," said Funt. "How unfortunate. I will call Pleća. She carries a first aid kit for these eventualities."

This is ridiculous, thought Devilly. It was merely a scratch.

"That will be unnecessary, Funt. I am all right. Just let me give this a little tug . . ."

Devilly gripped the end with a sucker and pulled. A thin stream of Devilly's green blood oozed into the water from the wound, while the black tip of the spine remained lodged in her flesh.

"Really, it is nothing."

"Pleća! Bring the first aid kit!"

"But I already have all the . . ."

By this time, the group had gathered around the edges of the pool. Pleća extracted a patch of new skin from the pouch she carried and applied it to the puncture.

"I am really quite fine," insisted Devilly, irritated by all the fuss.

"Still," said Funt. "I think it would be unwise to venture beyond the reef with an open wound."

"Hey Dev, that's too bad," added Tye. "You can wait on the edge of the reef when we do our dive. Those spines usually work their way out after a while. Pleća can stay with you."

"No, I will remain with Ms. Peen," said Funt, an ingratiating smile spreading across his features. "I am her Buddy, after all."

Chapter 18

OW OFTEN, THOUGHT Serafin Funt, had fortune smiled upon him? On all his projects—as he called them—he had benefited from a bit of luck. He prided himself that he was not one whose meticulous plans could not be adapted to changing circumstances. No, he expected contingencies; he welcomed them, relished the surprise turn of events.

Today was no exception. True, he had a Plan A, one that would ensure the demise of his victim. But he also left himself options; the reef excursion held so many possibilities. And that Tye Bondy was such a casual fool as trip leader, that an accident was almost bound to happen. Would happen.

When discussing the itinerary in his office the previous evening, all he had to do was authorize Tye's suggestion that the trip would be "a real hit" for the guests if *Ripples* would allow him to chum the waters beyond the outer reef.

"The clients want to see big fish, Mr. Funt."

"Our guests' safety must be our prime concern."

"It is safe! I set the bait in open water, and we watch from the reef. It's a winner, Mr. Funt."

"Well, if you are certain you can do it at no risk to our guests."

Sometimes, mulled Serafin to himself, sometimes it was almost too easy pulling the puppet strings.

"There are twelve going tomorrow, including that Ms. Peen. You will take special care of her? She is quite old."

"Dev? She's a feisty one. You should'a seen the old bag surfing."

✦ ✦ ✦

THE GROUP CLUNG to various nooks and crannies of the reef front. They were below the heavy churn of the waves, which were surging and sucking against the wall of coral. The sea was getting up, thought Serafin.

The deep divers had returned from their descent. It had been uneventful; the turbid water had limited visibility, and no one had spotted any exotic marine life. He heard mutterings about the reef being fished out, and where were the really cool corals?

He suckered smoothly over to Devilly.

"Ms. Peen, I think now might be a good moment, if you have the urn with you?"

His timing was perfect. Everyone was watching Bondy and that sullen squid Kalamarnica jetting away into open water, dragging the sack of offal behind them. He felt a delicious surge of anticipation.

"Perhaps, if we may move a little further away? I know a place where there is more current to carry the remains far out to sea."

Serafin began to feel that familiar tingling in his tentacles that presaged action. He had no doubts about his ability to overpower the elderly octo. He led the way around a corner to a gap in the coral wall where a broad funnel opened, leading into the heart of the reef. The water surged in and out restlessly to the beat of the waves.

"May I suggest releasing the contents when the wave retreats, Ms. Peen? The swell will waft Dr. McKelpie into deep water to sink gently to the abyss, as he would wish."

He watched as Devilly pulled the urn from the folds of her mantle.

"I would like to say a few words, Mr. Funt."

Of course, she bloody would. Serafin smiled deferentially and waited as Devilly muttered something about whiskey and second chances. She remained head-bowed for a full minute while he fidgeted.

"Ahem." He decided to move things along. "You must wait for the wave. Count one second, two seconds, three seconds." The water began to retreat.

He judged it was almost time. If only those fools would hurry up with the chum. He flexed his tentacles.

"Oh! Look at those fish!"

Serafin turned to see what had caught Devilly's attention. Out there, hanging in mid-water was the ball of bait. Around it circled several long shapes. At last!

"Sharks, Madam," he whispered, his voice husky with his desire to kill.

They watched the first shark bite and shake its head violently, releasing a cloud of blood into the water. Suddenly there was a maelstrom of fish, turning and twisting in frenzy.

✧   ✧   ✧

SHE WOULD DEFINITELY take a whiskey when she got back to *Ripples*, decided Devilly—a last farewell. Disposing of Sandy was a sad duty, but she imagined that adventures on package holidays always came to abrupt ends one way or another.

"Now!" She heard Funt shout over the background roar of water.

Devilly tipped the urn, and they watched the beak tumbling down and away with the retreating wave, swathed in a cloud of bubbles.

The next roller was coming in. She had counted to six, and this was the seventh. Tye's advice—she recalled from her introduction to surfing—was to wait for the seventh wave of the set; it was usually by far the biggest. This one promised to be a giant, what with the incoming tide and the rising wind. She already sensed its power. She tried to turn to sucker on to the coral rock, but Funt had gripped her from behind.

Devilly was helpless, dangled out from the reef like a lure. Funt ripped the bandage from her wound with one tentacle so that she bled into the water.

"The feeding frenzy is quite a spectacle, Ms. Peen. Perhaps you would care for a closer look."

Funt prepared to plunge his beak into the back of Devilly's head, a bite to sever the nerves controlling his victim's motor functions. This was the coup de grâce, the culmination, the sublime act, his misericord: his joy.

Devilly thrashed wildly with her tentacles. Funt's grip slipped, sliding off the Sunslime she had so liberally applied. She contracted violently, ejecting the contents of her mantle—her ink and all of her poison sac, including its reference collection of assorted venom. A cloud of poison enveloped Funt.

She felt the tentacles holding her twitch,

then relax. One puff from her jet, and she was against the wall of the reef, clinging for dear life while Funt hung suspended in mid channel, immobilized by the paralyzing cocktail.

The fool should have read some of her novels, thought Devilly fleetingly; knowing your victim's hobbies should be the first rule of a successful assassin. She watched as the bemused grin on Funt's face turn to a look of horror as he felt the tug of the incoming wave.

The current caught Funt, lifting him further up the narrowing funnel that led into the reef. Devilly's last glimpse of her assailant was of a tumbling ball of flesh, bouncing from side to side against its jagged coralline walls.

The seventh wave that swept past Devilly was followed by a deep trough that left her exposed, sprawled on the reef top. She heard a deep gurgling, as of a throat clearing, and swiveled towards the sound. For a brief second, she saw nothing in the tumult of foam. Then, with the force of an explosion, a column of seawater erupted into the sky. It was streaked with yellow and red—the shredded remains of Funt spat from the Devil's Blow Pipe.

The wind caught the plume, carrying the spray offshore. Minced Funt pattered onto the sea above the spot where Tye and Pleća had tethered the bag of chum. The surface boiled anew with this welcome addition to the menu.

Well, thought Devilly, it had been a complete waste of time trying to organize her reference collection of poisons. It is strange how in such moments one thinks of the most domestic things.

Chapter 19

Sergeant Caracol found Devilly clutching a coral stump. The sea was still washing in and out of the funnel, but the waves had diminished over the past few minutes: the water seemed confused, choppy, with less purpose, and the Pipe was merely squirting tentatively.

"Señora, you are safe!"

"Funt is gone, Sergeant! Dead! Taken by the Devil's Blow Pipe."

"*Santa María!*" said Caracol.

He gripped Devilly firmly and led her across the reef to rejoin the expedition gathered in the lee of a large brain coral. Pleća Kalamarnica saw Devilly first and finned to her side.

"Oh, Ms. Peen. I was so worried when we could not find you, and I guessed you had gone alone with Señor Funt. I warn you!"

"He tried to kill me, Pleća," whispered Devilly.

✧   ✧   ✧

HALF AN HOUR later, police officers were still attempting to cordon off the reef area. They had little success: waves kept ripping the tape free, streaming it back over the reef. A scene of crime officer was flailing with a plastic bag, trying to catch a sample of pink water.

Comandante Pesquero arrived and took charge. Apprised of the situation by Caracol, he had little confidence that forensics would be much help; lacking a body, analysis back at the lab might confirm Funt as the victim but finding a strand of his particular DNA in tropical seawater seemed unlikely. Besides, they had a witness.

Several of the tourists were in a state of shock and were being treated by paramedics. Most had been floating at the reef edge, relaxing after their dive when Funt rained down on them. At first, many assumed that the colourful fountain shooting from the Devil's

Blow Pipe was a natural phenomenon and applauded the spectacle. Now, after learning the truth, the Comandante watched them frantically swabbing fragments of the Assistant Manager from their skin.

The tide was coming in quickly now. Looking out from the reef front, the Comandante could see that the sharks had begun to swim closer, anticipating the moment when they could venture across the reef to hunt. He judged they could do little more out here on the barrier. At high water, waves would roll clear across the reef; all evidence of Funt would be washed away, to be filtered by the corals or consumed by the voracious crustaceans that would emerge in swarms from myriad crannies.

Pesquero took out a whistle and blew three bubbling notes to recall his men. He turned to address the group huddled behind the coral head.

"Señor Bondy? The current in the channel is favourable. It is unwise to linger. Now, we must all return to *Ripples*."

✧ ✧ ✧

HAVING CONDUCTED DEVILLY safely back through the lagoon and installed her in the cafeteria, Comandante Pesquero was at his most solicitous.

"Shock, Señora," he explained. "It comes in many forms. You must not concern yourself more."

He signaled to his sergeant to bring Devilly a cup of tea. She was shivering: the swim through the warm waters of the lagoon had done nothing to ease the chill that had pervaded her body.

"I keep seeing his face. The look of terror."

"It will pass, Señora."

"But how did you know about Funt, Comandante? I tried but couldn't leave you a message."

Pesquero explained that the police had raided the Barrio, where they arrested several members of the *Los Picos* gang. It had taken time—the good sergeant's methods being slow but effective—but one *pico* had finally admitted that he took night classes given by Señor

Funt on techniques of assassination. Apparently, some of the more ambitious and literate undesirables attended regularly. Furthermore, Major Siphon, in a bottlegram from the Gyre had provided information to confirm Funt's dubious activities. He had discovered that Funt had worked at all the *Ochas Lagunas* resorts over the past seven years. On each occasion, one of the wealthier guests had died in a presumed accident. The police had no reason to suspect foul play.

"So, I confess, Señora," said Pesquero, "that my suspicions of Señor McKelpie were unfounded."

"Well, I knew it couldn't be poor Sandy," replied Devilly. "I began to suspect Funt when I saw his handwriting on the blackboard in the lobby and compared it to the note I received, supposedly from McKelpie. I remembered when we first arrived at *Ripples*, Sandy told me that he recognized Funt from somewhere, and Funt probably recognized him. But I reasoned that, once having disposed of McKelpie, he would have no reason to kill me."

"He must have assumed that McKelpie had

told you of his suspicions. He knew who you were friends."

"We were not friends..." began Devilly. She sighed. "But I think in the end, Sandy saved my life. His prescription for Sunslime was water resistant and very effective: Funt just couldn't get a grip. In a way, I suppose Sandy had his revenge on his own murderer."

"Bravo, Señora. I am sure this experience will inspire your next work. I will look forward to reading it."

"Yes," said Devilly, "and I am sure you will feature in it, Comandante."

"*Obligado*, Señora. I would be most honoured."

True, thought Devilly, she had not worried about her writing drought during her stay at *Ripples*. But what material for Daisy Cuttle to get her teeth into when she returned to Nether Vortex!

Chapter 20

DEVILLY WAS RELUCTANT to pay for a taxi from the jetport all the way home; the outgoing trip had cost a fortune in clams. Instead, she opted for the shuttle to Gyre Centro. It departed every twenty minutes and cost a fraction of the price. From there, she could catch the stopping train to Nether Vortex.

The downtown streets seemed somehow bleaker than she remembered; the serried windows of the bottle apartments, block after block, lacked the variety of the lagoon. Even the slummy areas of Tire Town had managed a certain vibrancy.

Descending from the shuttle at the downtown terminus, she joined the lunchtime crowds of office workers hurrying to buy a quick lunch. Jetting swiftly to keep up with the flow, she passed the display windows of stores that had all agreed, it seemed, to carry only the tope and beige of this year's autumn fashion.

She turned left at the towering PlastiBank building, that pop-styled monument to the ego of an architect Devilly despised. Then a right onto narrower streets leading away from the commercial bustle. It was not far now.

Tired from the exertion of trailing her sack for what felt like miles, she finally arrived at Police Headquarters. Devilly wanted to apprise her nephew of recent events. She had sent him a postcard soon after arriving at Ripples, but there were some things better discussed in person. "Beach wonderful, water warm and exciting seafood, love Auntie" didn't really do justice to her holiday. Even the bit about the seafood needed qualifying.

"So, Aunt, a bit of a bus driver's holiday, by the sound of it." Moray had installed his relative in the comfortable chair in his office and provided her with a desperately needed cup of tea. He was listening attentively.

"Yes, I remember my old boss mentioning Major Siphon. Gone into insurance, has he? Well, it takes all sorts."

"He expects MerryVac to tighten background checks on policy owners and their beneficiaries. He wants to believe that Funt was operating alone, a deranged loner, for all his bonhomie."

"It sounds plausible," said the Inspector.

"But I think Funt can't have been acting alone. Surely there had to be an accomplice, someone to identify candidates for the scam. That person would not be on the island, but on the Gyre. When I mentioned this to Lionel Siphon, he insisted that Funt's death closed the case."

"It is strange that he should disregard the possibility," mused Moray. "I would expect him to jump at the chance of uncovering a mole in the MerryVac organization. That would be right up his street. Perhaps he doesn't want to share the credit with you."

"He was quite rude about Daisy Cuttle."

"That's it then. I expect he his trawling through the MerryVac database as we speak, looking for anomalies."

"Oh well. I suppose that's enough excitement for me. *Ochas Lagunas* promised a dream vacation at *Ripples*. They delivered: it turned out to be an all-inclusive with a vengeance."

Devilly put down her teacup and made to rise.

"I have taken up too much of your time. You must be busy."

"No, not particularly. But I suppose I should tackle that mound of paper." Moray glanced ruefully at the mountain of damp files in the corner of his office.

"So, what now, Aunt?" he asked, escorting her to the elevator.

"Back to Nether Vortex and the rumours of Margo Seethe-Mantle's affair with the vicar."

"I am sure you will sort that out in no time," said her nephew with a smile.

✧　✧　✧

DEVILLY DID NOT have to wait long for a train. The 4:15 to the outer Gyre departed just before the rush hour out of Centro began, and it was usually possible to find a nook. The doors hissed shut and the familiar voice of the conductor came on to remind passengers to grip securely prior to departure. As they accelerated, the sucking of the vacuum tube bore in on Devilly that she was back in civilization.

Leaving the suburbs of Centro, the countryside flattens, a monotonous scene of fields of plastic bottles stretching to the horizon. Only the occasional mound of erect plastic rose above the plain, marking towns and villages that Devilly could identify by name. It was dull, but somehow comforting. It was home.

By the time she popped from the tube at the station, the sun was low on the horizon. The venerable plastic of the church tower glowed pink in the last of its oblique rays, but below water all was shadow. After the warmth of *Isla Florida*, she felt quite chilly. No one was there to meet her—she had cut her holiday short by three days. As she dragged her sack along the lane leading to the grottage, Devilly feared the worst.

Lawrence had neglected the garden. The coral was terminally bleached by the look of it, and a posse of grazing limpets were invading the anemone bed. It would take serious weed-ing. Still, much seemed as she had left it, although some of her papers lay in disorder, testimony to Lawrence's inept tidying up. A few bottles rolled on the floor, delivered—Devilly supposed—through the chute in the front door. This happened occasionally when the mail pool got overly congested, and the bottle man had to make the rounds. She sorted the post absentmindedly. The brown bottles would be bills; the plastic flyers from estate agents bragging of property sold near Nether Vortex at ridiculous prices, and here the parish magazine in its flimsy wrapping—a five minute read at best.

The garish stamp on one bottle caught her eye. She grabbed it with a sucker and examined the postmark. Why was she receiving mail from *Isla Florida*? Then she realized the addressee was Lawrence Clutnife.

It is easy to extract a message from an unopened bottle with a tentacle. Devilly had developed the technique so Daisy Cuttle could discover the true relationship of Anguilla Waters to her son Algo in *The Clasper*, now ranked disappointingly at 128th in cozy mystery.

She applied herself to the task and soon extracted the scroll of plastic inside. It was a note.

Cousin. I have removed the inconvenience mentioned previously. That fellow had recognized me from another resort. Now I can focus on our original plan. By the time you receive this, I will have finished the job. I trust you have found the MerryVac policy and made sure she has named you as beneficiary. With luck, you will continue to receive the wretched woman's royalties. This promises to be our most profitable undertaking! S.F.

S.F.? Serafin Funt! Of course. But this meant that it was she, Devilly, who had been the object of the insurance scam all along, not Sandy McKelpie. She barely remembered even having an insurance policy, and for the life of her could not imagine who she had written in as beneficiary. Moray, probably, as her closest living relative.

Lionel Siphon mentioned that Funt used the name "Funticle" at other *Ochas Lagunas* resorts. And, and—all of Devilly's brains were singing in febrile concert—wasn't Clutnife an anagram of Funticle? Lawrence Clutnife was Lawrence Funticle! He was the shape-shifting cousin of Serafin Funt, a would-be actor who pretended to despise physical metamorphosis and had opted for role play as much less exhausting.

✧   ✧   ✧

DEVILLY SETTLED IN her writing nook. She had contacted Moray again and could rely on the Inspector to make the appropriate arrangements. Luckily, the local constabulary was only minutes away. Taking out her long-neglected knitting—something for Moray's first polp— she settled down to wait for Lawrence's return. As a precaution, she had selected her sharpest needles and coated the tips with a strong muscle relaxant. It had been a relief to find her favourite cone shell relatively docile. It permitted Devilly to extract a sufficient dose of venom while cautiously stroking its foot. She did not expect to have to resort to spearing

Lawrence, but it was best to be prepared: she was not sure of what the youth might be capable.

She looked at the time. He should be here at any minute after his rehearsal. What play were they doing? Some farce or other. She really didn't care. But perhaps that was a fiction too? She remembered Lawrence had mentioned working in insurance. Could he be interning at MerryVac? That would give him access to the files, and the opportunity to forge his name on the company records.

Devilly set aside the knitting, and prepared tea, and then remembered the package she had left on the hall table. It had arrived at *Ripples* on the morning of her departure. Pleća Kalamarnica—newly promoted because of the recent staff vacancy—had been on the reception desk and had run after her.

"For you Ms. Peen. This has just arrived."

"Thank you Pleća. And thank you for an exciting holiday. I hope next time you are on the Gyre, you will come visit me in Nether Vortex. And good luck with your thesis!"

"Oh, Ms. Peen. Will you sign?" She had held

out a copy of *Club Murder*. "I practice my English."

What a charming and outgoing girl she was!

Now, back home, Devilly tore open the padded envelope and extracted the sealed packet from Monsieur Le Pieuff's emporium. The instructions cautioned against exceeding the prescribed dose: only a small teaspoonful would suffice to induce hysterical convulsions. She filled a tea strainer and placed it on the tray beside Lawrence's cup.

Devilly glanced at her watch; nearly six and Lawrence had still failed to show. The mail being what it was, Lawrence must surely be unaware of his cousin's fate on the barrier reef of *Isla Florida*. She knew that he had unfinished business at the grottage: her MerryVac policy lay undisturbed along with other important documents in the garden shed under Grunt, her pet stonefish. To forge his name as beneficiary on her copy, he would first have to find it.

Devilly had brought out her back list to consult. There was a question of combining some titles in a box set. Lawrence, in his role as agent, should express an opinion. She would make him squirm like a worm on a hook until the police arrived.

She felt the faint pressure as someone pushed open the door. The crinoid flowers in the pot on the table bowed to the slight current. Devilly tensed.

"Madam Peen? Are you there?"

It was not Lawrence.

"Major Siphon!"

"Perhaps you were expecting Lawrence Clutnife, or rather Funticle? He won't be joining us, I'm afraid. Clever young fellow: less of a psychopath than his older cousin, but just as unlucky."

Devilly dropped her knitting. Had she missed something; had some clue escaped her? To cover her confusion, she swept a tentacle towards the pile of plastic bottles that served as an armchair.

"Well, this is a surprise, Lionel. Won't you sit? Will you have some tea?'

"Have some of *your* tea?" Siphon looked amused." I don't think that would be wise, do you?"

"What have you done with Lawrence?"

"Gone for a swim. Straight down. He should be reaching the abyss about now. Do you know how long it takes a weighted octopod to sink?"

"So, you knew about the Funts all along?"

"Not at all: I was convinced it was McKelpie. Funt took me by surprise. Only later did I realize you must be right about the accomplice."

"Is that why you came back to the Gyre so quickly?"

Keep him talking, thought Devilly. That is what Daisy would do.

"Yes. When I got back to MerryVac, it didn't take me long to work out that it must be your Lawrence and that you were their next target. I could have laughed."

"But why, Lionel?"

"Why? Because you are worth five million clams to me. That is what MerryVac will pay out. I'm afraid I told you a little fib, Devilly. That Clamshucker business put paid to my career. MerryVac has me on a retainer, and a bonus only when I catch someone trying to cheat. This way I get the bonus, and I profit from the Funt's original plan."

"But that means you will have to alter the beneficiary again."

"Of course, and we'll do that together in a minute. Lawrence couldn't find your policy, and he spent days searching for it. There is one place he didn't look, of course."

"Really?"

"Yes, you told me back at Ripples. Where you keep things safe, and no one would dare to look. Where is Grunt, by the way? In the garden shed, is he?"

"I don't see how you are going to get away with this."

"Accidents happen, my dear Devilly. And your stonefish has a reputation. MerryVac has compensated for five deaths from stonefish encounters in the past year. That is one less than the average. Yours will balance the statistics."

The bubbling wail of a police siren interrupted Siphon. He jetted to the door and looked up and down the lane. The distant sound died. Satisfied, he returned to Devilly and pulled a syringe from his cloak.

"A paralytic," he said, seeing Devilly's glance. "As you would know, there are several options which disappear rapidly from the bloodstream."

Devilly made to jet through the door into the garden, but Siphon intercepted her and pulled her backwards, his tentacle raised to inject his victim. They both sprawled onto the pile of bottles where Devilly had been sitting a moment before.

"Argh! What was that?" Siphon released Devilly and struggled to free himself of the clinging plastic. He reached back and tugged free a long spine from where it had lodged in his mantle. He stared at it, stupefied.

"Oh, that is one of my knitting needles. Thank you for retrieving it."

The wail of the siren was much louder now, cutting off abruptly just outside. A moment later, Moray appeared at the door, followed by two uniformed officers.

"Siphon, move away from my aunt and spread your tentacles!"

But Siphon, speared by agony, had already released Devilly and was floating in the middle of the room immobile, his tentacles locked in tetany.

"Moray, you took your time," Devilly reproached her nephew. "I had to take matters into my own tentacles. Major Siphon appears to have stabbed himself with a needle tipped with cone shell poison. It is not invariably fatal."

Chapter 21

"**I** CHECKED. SIPHON left the force under a cloud, suspected of receiving bribes. I suppose he falsified his references and must have seemed a good catch for MerryVac, what with his experience in Special Branch."

Inspector Moray was sitting in the garden with his Aunt Devilly. They were drinking a sherry to celebrate. His men had removed Lionel Siphon, who would spend many days in intensive care before being moved to a cell. Moray would have preferred to get back to the station and start the paperwork, but Devilly insisted he remain behind.

"I've had a shock, you know, Moray. I am not as young as I used to be."

"Believe me, Aunt, I think this holiday has perked you up. You went surfing, I believe?"

"Yes, well. That was a mistake," admitted

Devilly. "But about the Funts, did you look into their background?"

"Yes. Funt had an uncle who died together with his wife, leaving her son Lawrence in foster care. Our profiler has this theory that Funt groomed his cousin over several years. The money he won from the insurance seems to have paid for Lawrence to go to Drama School."

"So that wasn't all a lie?"

"Not at all. I saw Lawrence performing at the Fringe in Centro last week. He was quite good, for a metamorph."

They sipped their sherry in silence for a minute.

"Well, Aunt, I really must be off," said Moray. "I take it you won't be taking another holiday off the Gyre any time soon."

"Well, there is a young fellow called Tide-water Bondy I met at *Ripples* who is planning an arctic expedition."

"What? Oh, you're joking. I should think you have enough material to keep you busy. You had a close call this time. If we hadn't arrived . . ."

"Oh, I would have been fine. Thank Good-
ness for poisonous snails."

The End

Other titles by E.K Wicher

"The Gyre" – A Devilly Peen Murder Mystery

"The Leda" – A novel of landslides and small towns

"The Blackwater Sailing Club" – A novel of mild dystopia, of sailing and Quebec politics

Ekwicher.com